To Love, Finding its Way

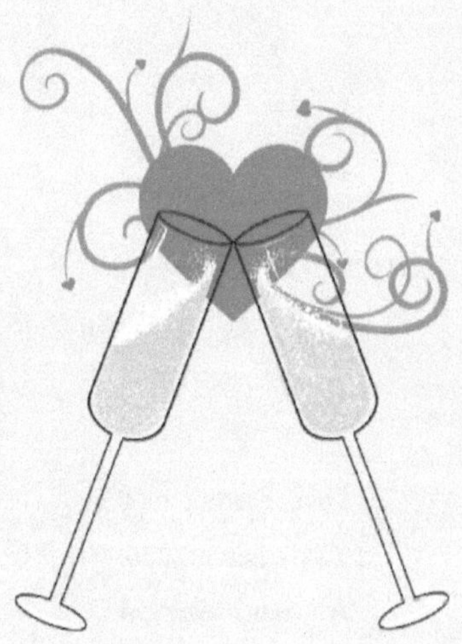

By

Alexandria Chiaro

To Love, Finding its Way

Paperback ISBN: 979-8-9873179-6-9

E-Book ASIN: B0GMY6JBZS

Cover Design and Illustrations by Gretchen Caughey

Dedication

A heart of gratitude and thankfulness to

Our Father in Heaven.

To my family, my friends, and life's hiccups.

To Inspirations that hit out of the blue,

Or those that have been long burning....

I hope you enjoy this story

CHAPTER 1

One Day...I'll Marry That Girl

The first week of May offers a day full of sunshine for the final track meet of the year. Nick finishes his stretches along with the other high school boys on the track team. He glances around and views the field. It quickly becomes embodied with kids from six different schools.

"Come on, Nick. We need to get over to the hurdles." Alex motions.

Nick stands and nods.

Nick and Alex are some distance behind the other teammates. Nick continues to scan around when he sees her. A tall girl with long brunette hair that is banded up in a ponytail. It does not matter to Nick if he perhaps is not quite as tall. He is determined to meet her.

"Hey, I'll catch up to you." Nick darts away from Alex.

"Wait! Where are you going? We need to get to our places," Alex hollers with his arms out to his sides.

Nick signals with his hand. "I won't be late! I'll be right there!"

Nick sprints to catch up to the girl that captures his attention.

Nick slows his run to walk. His adjusts his stride, so it is in unison next to the girl and her teammates. "Hi there." Nick tries to be smooth, though he is completely nervous.

"Hey." The girl with the long hair in a ponytail, smiles.

"My name is Nick. I go to this school. So, I see by your shirt you are from Liberty?" Nick strikes up a conversation.

"Hi. My name is Nicole. Yes, we go to Liberty High in Careyville," Nicole informs.

"Wow! What a coincidence that our names are similar! Are you a senior?" Nick inquires.

"I am." Nicole's face hosts a smile she cannot wipe off. Attention from this unknown, handsome, long-legged boy sparks her interest.

"That's cool. I am a senior as well. Are you going to college?" Nick asks.

"I am planning on it. I plan to go to the state university. I have a scholarship," Nicole informs.

The two straggle a little behind the girls she is walking with.

Nick turns his head to peer into Nicole's eyes and notices they are piercing blue. "That's impressive. What's your major?"

"Math." Nicole slightly laughs. "I just like math. So, we will see what I do with it."

"Does that mean you are going to keep in contact with me?" Nick does not miss an opening.

"What?" Nicole laughs again and wonders, *who is this boy that can make me laugh?*

"You said 'WE will see,' so…I am wondering if that means you and me?" Nick grins.

Nicole laughs again and shakes her head. "No silly, well maybe…I don't know. You have me confused now."

"Aw, I don't think you're confused at all," Nick confidently assures.

Again, his ability to make her laugh, impresses Nicole.

The seniors arrive near the end of the field and see their teams.

Nick and Nicole face each other.

"I guess I better go." Nicole gazes into the brown eyes of Nick.

"Good luck, today. I hope I can see you again," Nick conveys.

"I would like that." Nicole smiles.

Nick reaches out with his hand to shake the hand of Nicole.

"What's this?" Nicole raises an eyebrow.

"It's called a handshake," Nick explains. A curious expression crosses his face. "It's what people do when they meet people."

Nicole giggles and grins. "I know. I just wanted to hear your voice."

Now-Nick blushes. "I like that."

"I thought you would." Nicole smiles, tilts her head, bites her lower lip, and dashes off.

Nick hollers, "I'll be seeing you?"

"All day!" Nicole stops to holler back.

Nick takes a few steps in her direction. "Can I get your phone number?"

"Yes! Find me after your race." Nicole smiles.

Nick smiles and nods, he then gestures a salute.

Nicole nods, turns, and darts to her teammates.

CHAPTER 2

Getting to Know You/Growing to Love You

On the first Saturday after graduation, which is mid-May, Nick drives to Careyville to visit Nicole and meet her family. He feels very welcome by her family.

During the meal, the Thompson parents subject Nick to all the usual interrogation queries they reserve for their daughters' suitors. Nick is a good sport and understands Nicole's family is very tightknit. Nicole's parents, Seth and Laurie Thompson, appear to enjoy Nick's company.

"Nicole's older sisters will be home in a few weeks, why don't you come back in two Saturdays," Seth invites Nick.

"I would be honored, sir." Nick smiles. "Would Nicole be allowed to come to my home next weekend? My parents would like to meet all of you, if you would be willing to drive to our place."

Seth and Laurie glance at each other. "That is a very thoughtful idea. We look forward to it!"

"Excellent!" Nick relays. "My parents will love that!"

"Very good. Be sure to write your address and directions down before you leave today," Seth mentions.

"Of course!" Nick nods.

Nick enjoys the rest of the day with Nicole and her family.

Nicole escorts him out to his car when it is time to leave. Nick parked his car on the tree canopied brick street next to the curb in front of the Thompson home.

"I sure do like you, Nicole." Nick slightly tilts his head and smiles.

Nicole's smile is painted on her face. "I am glad you do! I like you, too! And I love your voice!"

Nick grins. "Okay, I'll be seeing you."

"Yes! Next Saturday morning we will drive over and spend the day! Can I bring my best friend, Cami?" Nicole asks.

"Well, sure. I will invite my best friend, Alex." Nick reaches to open his car door.

"I look forward to meeting him! Will Cami like him?" Nicole asks.

"Probably. Everyone loves Alex," Nick responds. "Can I hug you goodbye?"

"I would like that." Nicole blushes.

The two awkward teenagers open their arms toward each other, navigating themselves into each other's arms.

"I can get used to this!" Nick grins.

"Yeah, you hug nice, smell good, and I LOVE your voice!" Nicole behaves giddy.

"Okay, I will see you, Cami, and your parents Saturday at my house," Nick confirms.

"Yes!" Nicole stands up on her tiptoes and then back down.

Nick gets into his car.

"Wait!" Nicole smiles and gently taps on his window.

Nick rolls down his window. "What? Is everything alright?"

Nicole playfully grins. "I just wanted to hear your voice."

"Aww, you're sweet." Nick grins. "Okay, I'll see you for sure Saturday, if not before."

"Drive safe! Call me when you get home." Nicole waves.

Nick affirms, "I will do that.

Saturday rolls around. Seth, Laurie, Nicole, and Cami, step into Seth's truck and drive about an hour to the home of Nick and his family.

"He gave us good directions," Seth comments.

"Oh, look at this place! Just spectacular! I love these trees that line their driveway!" Laurie counts. "There are twelves trees on each side. Oh, Seth, if we ever move again, let's find a place in the country!"

Seth grins. "We can do that."

"They're here!" Nick opens the door from the garage into the house and hollers at his parents. Nick and Alex come out from garage to greet them.

Emily and Paul step out of their front door, down the steps, and across the sidewalk over to the driveway. After the family gets out of their truck, Paul approaches Seth and extends his hand to shake Seth's hand. "Hello, I am Paul Parks, this is my wife, Emily, you know Nick, and this is his best friend, Alex."

Seth and Paul exchange a firm handshake. Laurie, Cami, and Nicole step close to everyone.

"Hello, I am Emily." Emily also reaches to shake the hand of Laurie.

"Nice to meet you." Laurie firmly shakes Emily's hand and smiles. "This is our youngest daughter, Nicole, and her best friend, Cami."

"So nice you could make it! How soon do you have to be home?" Emily asks.

"We usually attend Mass at five p.m.," Nicole answers.

"Oh, well…why don't you join us at our parish this evening? That way you do not have to rush home," Emily suggests.

Laurie glances over to Seth.

Seth nods.

"Alright, sounds lovely." Laurie follows Emily across the sidewalk to the front porch.

"Very well," Emily voices. She steps to open the door for their guests. Norie is standing in the foyer. "And this is our daughter, Nick's younger sister, Norie."

"Very nice to meet you. Are you…maybe fifteen?" Laurie smiles.

"How did you know?" Norie asks.

"I have three daughters." Laurie winks.

Norie's eyes light up. "How fun!"

"It is! My two older girls are at college and Nicole heads out in August," Laurie makes conversation with Norie.

"Don't you miss them?" Norie quizzes.

"Terribly." Laurie reaches out and places her right hand on Norie's left arm.

The families and best friends enjoy an incredible day in the country. The food that Paul and Emily serve is scrumptious. The Thompsons very much enjoy their day and Mass.

"I love your parish! It feels like home!" Nicole voices.

Emily smiles. "Ya know, we felt the very same thing the first time we attended this parish."

After Mass, the families and best friends visit outside the parish.

"Our older daughters will be home in two weeks. Why don't you all join us at our place. We can go to the lake. We have a boat. We can go boating and even skiing if you all want," Seth proposes.

Paul and Emily exchange a quick glance at each other.

"We look forward to it. Do I need to bring some extra life jackets?" Paul inquires.

"I think we have enough, but you are welcome to bring a few." Seth nods.

The families say their farewells and depart. On the return drive to Careyville, Laurie and Seth comment how much they enjoy the Parks family. Nicole and Cami giggle in the backseat.

Nicole lights up when she hears how much her parents enjoy Nick's family.

Over the course of the rest of May, all of June, and July, the families spend time getting to know each other. Nick and Nicole, along with their best friends, also schedule time together without their parents and siblings. They enjoy a variety of activities from eating at the best hamburger hangout or pizza place. They go fishing at the lake near Nick's home. Golfing, bowling, tennis, and movies are also some activities the high school graduates take pleasure in. The time they spend with their families include cookouts, boating, skiing, and game nights. The families enjoy bonding through activities paired with meaningful conversations and laughter. The families also attend Mass together in whichever town they are visiting. The summer days and weekends are filled with Nick and Nicole, along with their families, and best friends, getting to know each other.

"Ya know, this is the last day we will be able to hang out at the lake together… or anywhere for a while." Nicole ponders.

"I know. Time will pass by quickly. I'll be joining you at college shortly after you arrive up there, and then we will be studying." Nick laughs.

"You know what I want to do together?" Nicole questions.

Nick shakes his head. "No."

"I want us to travel to the mountains! I will show you all the cool places I have been! We can hike to the river's edge where the pine trees tower and the eagles soar. Where the colors of the aspen trees decorate the fall, and the trails lead to somewhere," Nicole lovingly voices.

"I look forward to that!" Nick assures.

"Yeah, me too." Nicole smiles. "Tell me a story," Nicole requests.

"A story? You'd like that?" Nick asks.

"Yes! Your voice calms me. It gives me peace when I hear it," Nicole reveals.

Nick feels honored. "I'm glad to hear that!" He wraps his arm around Nicole and they stroll down the path to the lake's edge. "Let me think…there was once a VERY handsome track star, who happened to be a senior in high school. At the last track meet of the season…."

Nicole giggles.

Nick continues to tell the best story he knows; the story of how they met.

Nicole lies back on the picnic table which is shaded by the decade's old cottonwood tree. She positions her arms behind her head, and rests her head onto her palms. She draws her legs toward her, so her knees are bent, resting her feet flat on the table. Nick sits on the bench of the table. He continues to narrate the story. Nicole enjoys listening to his words while in the background she hears the gentle waves of the lake splash against the shore. His voice truly soothes her spirit. Nicole turns her head to gaze upon Nick.

"You know, I am sweet on you." Nick pats the leg of Nicole.

Nicole smiles. "And I just wanted to hear your voice." Nicole, feeling overwhelming closeness and affection, peers into the eyes of Nick. "How does the story end?"

"Oh, it doesn't end. But the chapter ends with…." Nick pulls his legs from under the picnic table bench he is sitting on. Nick stands and leans over Nicole. He gently presses his lips onto hers. They savor in their kiss.

"I like the end of that chapter." Nicole stares up into Nick's eyes.

"I do, too. You realize, we do not even need words to communicate." Nick smiles, knowing not only is he sweet on Nicole, he plans to marry her.

"I know. Sitting in quiet with you is peaceful. Not awkward at all," Nicole assures, peering up at Nick.

"Unspoken words I see in your eyes are all the words I need to hear," Nick quietly professes.

"Wow. A poetic romantic…." Nicole grins.

"Not really…you just stir something inside me," Nick confides.

Nick and Nicole speak with their eyes, while they listen to the gentle waves splash against the shoreline.

CHAPTER 3

A Phone Call Away

"Did you call her?" Alex asks Nick as they make their way toward their vehicles.

"I did. My family and I are going to drive over Saturday and have dinner with her family before she leaves for college Sunday," Nick informs.

"Cool. Is that when you are going to ask her to marry you? What about college?" Alex questions.

"Yes. I plan to," Nick announces. "I want you as our best man."

Alex grins. "I'm in! I like her! This has been a great summer, hanging out with her and her friend, Cami. Nicole's sisters and parents are pretty cool, too."

"Yeah, it has been a great summer. And yes, I like everyone I have met," Nick declares. "We will go to college together, live in the married dorms, or rent a house. We will figure it out. Her parents gave me their blessing when I asked their permission."

Alex pats Nick's upper arm. "I'm happy for you."

"Thanks, man." Nick grins.

The best friends get into their own cars and leave the parking lot of the best burger joint, the Drummer Boy.

CHAPTER 4

Sirens

Paul, Nick's father, hears chatter on his radio scanner. He gets up from of his chair to take the scanner out of the family room and into the privacy of his office.

Paul rushes from his office, grabs his jacket, and reaches for his keys.

Nick's family hear sirens. They quickly move to their living room window to view out. They see emergency vehicles sailing by.

"What's happened?" Emily questions her husband.

Paul steps over to kiss his wife's cheek and whispers, "It doesn't sound good. I'll be back." Paul glances at his children, Nick, and Norie.

"Can I go with you, Dad?" Nick inquires.

"I don't think so," Paul states.

"Why not. You usually let me go. I am a volunteer," Nick pleads his case.

Paul glances at his wife.

Emily blinks and barely nods with approval.

"Get your jacket. We need to leave." Paul allows Nick to accompany him.

Nick and Paul climb into Paul's red Ram truck. They close their doors and buckle up.

"There is a serious wreck just past the bridge where the highway curves," Paul quietly discloses to his son, as he drives out of their long gravel driveway.

They are about five minutes away from the main highway.

"I pray they live," Nick solemnly communicates.

"I do too, son." Paul reaches over to Nick and gives him a pat.

As they approach the scene of the crash, a chill surges through Nick when he sees flashing lights. He scans the area. He spies a car spun around in the median, then he views a truck upside-down in the ditch. Anxiety instantly fills his brain.

"Dad?" Nick panics.

Paul slows and pulls safely onto the shoulder and parks. "Nick, you don't need to get out."

"Dad…." Nick panics and cries. "That looks like…." Nick gets out of the truck.

Paul closes his door after he steps out of his truck. Paul surveys the scene. He catches a glimpse of his son running down the shoulder and into the ditch. Paul chases after his son. He recognizes the truck.

Emergency crews are on the scene.

Paul catches up to Nick and places his arm around him while he stands beside him.

"It's Alex!" Nick cries out!

"The rescue workers know what they're doing," Paul quietly assures.

"I can't lose my best friend! He is going to be my best man!" Nick claims.

Paul sighs. "I know."

"That's why we were going to their home tomorrow…I was going to ask Nicole in front of all of you. I already have her parent's blessing…." Nick wipes his nose.

"Yes, of course. Your mother and I are very happy for you! She is a lovely young lady," Paul reaffirms approval.

The two continue to intensely observe the jaws of life and the rescue of Alex.

"Dad, I love Nicole. I know I have not spent even a year with her, but I plan to marry her someday…hopefully this fall," Nick anxiously reveals. He makes conversation to help balance the shock of the wreck.

Paul pats Nick in the middle of his back. "Your mother and I look forward to having Nicole as our daughter-in-law."

Paul and Nick witness Alex being pulled from his vehicle. EMS places Alex securely on the stretcher. Nick rushes to the ambulance.

"Is he alive?" Nick quizzes.

"He is…." Doug, one of the EMS paramedics, states.

"Can I ride back here with him? He is my best friend," Nick begs.

Doug glances over to Paul.

Paul nods. Paul whispers to Nick, "Stay out of their way."

"I will. I just must be with him," Nick attests.

"I will meet you at the hospital." Paul turns and treks over to discuss some details with the responders. He witnesses paramedics remove the other driver from the car in the median. Paul moves briskly to catch up with them. As he approaches, he notices a young woman, probably in her late twenties.

"Hello. My name is Paul Parks. I am the fire chief. When is your baby due?" Paul questions.

"Three weeks." The young woman manages to catch her breath to answer.

Paul takes a hold of her hand while he walks next to the stretcher. "You're in good hands. What is your name?"

"Amy. Amy Chambers," The young woman voices between contractions.

Paul gathers information from the young lady before she is placed in the back of the ambulance.

"Just talking to you has calmed me. Thank you." Amy barely smiles.

"I am glad to be of service, Amy. You take care of your baby and you," Paul conveys.

Amy nods between sniffles. "I will."

The paramedics load Amy into the back of the ambulance. They head to the hospital.

Nick squeezes Alex's hand in the ambulance, and then releases his hand. He does not want to be in the way of the paramedics. Nick quietly, unceasingly prays for his friend and whoever was in the other vehicle. Great anxiety sweeps through every fiber of Nick, but he remains vigilant in prayer.

The ambulance finally arrives at a nearby hospital. The back doors fling open.

Nick leans in close to whisper, "You're gonna be alright, buddy. Hang in there! Remember, we have a wedding…."

A second team assists the paramedics to move Alex from the ambulance. Together, they transport Alex inside the emergency room. Nick crawls out behind the crew and anxiously follows. They rush Alex into the emergency surgical care unit.

"Nick, will you please give the registration staff information until his parents arrive," Doug requests.

"I will." Nick nods.

Paul arrives at the hospital shortly thereafter, and enters the emergency room. He finds his son pacing.

"Alex's parents should arrive any time. The sheriff went to their home to notify them in person," Paul communicates.

Nick states, "I need to call Nicole and tell her we will not be driving to her see her and her family tomorrow."

"Are you sure?" Paul asks.

"Dad…Alex and I have been best friends since preschool. I am not leaving his side. Nicole will understand," Nick asserts.

Paul nods and pats his son on his back.

"I'm going to use the phone and call Nicole," Nick informs.

Paul nods.

Nick relocates over to the courtesy phone and dials Nicole's home phone number.

"Hello?" Nicole answers.

Nick becomes choked up with emotion. "Nicole?"

"Yes. Nick?" Nicole voices concern.

Tears form in Nick's eyes. His nose begins to drip. Nicole can hear his sniffles.

"Nick. What's happened? What's wrong?" Nicole panics.

"He's hurt bad," Nick can barely speak. He gasps for breath. "Alex. It's Alex. He was in a bad wreck," Nick reveals.

Nicole feels shock. She is silent.

"I don't know what to do. I have been praying for him non-stop," cries Nick. "My parents and I won't be able to come over and have dinner with you and your family tomorrow. I am so sorry. I wanted to see you the day before you leave for college."

"Oh, Nick! No, do not come! You *need* to be with Alex and his family. I am just sorry I am not there with you." Nicole sighs. She feels helpless.

Paul walks over to his son. He places one hand on Nick's arm while he gently reaches his other hand to take the phone from Nick's hand.

"Nicole?" Paul asks.

"Yes," Nicole replies.

"This is Paul, Nick's father. Nick will call you later. We are waiting to hear from the surgeon," Paul expresses.

"Oh, yes. Certainly. I understand," Nicole conveys.

Nicole bolts down the stairs into the kitchen as soon as the summer sun shines through her window. "Dad, Mom, may I please drive to the hospital over in Grant? I want to be there for Nick, and see Alex. I mean, I leave for college tomorrow. It would not feel right-not going to see them!"

Nicole's parents, Seth and Laurie, glance at each other.

"I tell you what...your mother and I discussed this situation last night after you told us what happened. We have decided we will come with you," Seth states.

"Thank you. That is probably a good idea." Nicole nods.

"How soon can you be ready?" Laurie asks.

"Five minutes!" Nicole dashes up the stairs to her bedroom. She puts on an appropriate dress and a pair of heels. She begins to leave her bedroom when she thinks to herself, *I will be on my feet all day. I will wear tennis shoes.*

She slides her dress shoes off, sets them on a shelf, and pulls out a comfortable pair of sneakers. She looks in the full-length mirror, tosses her hair, rushes to the bathroom to quickly brush her teeth. She reaches for some lip balm and applies it to her lips. She tosses the balm on the counter while she races out of the bathroom.

Seth, Laurie, and Nicole, load up in the truck and set out for the hospital in Grant City.

CHAPTER 5

At the Hospital

Seth backs his truck into a stall in the crowded parking lot of the hospital. The Thompson family step out of the truck and move with purpose to the automatic, double doors of the hospital, and enter. Seth approaches the counter. He asks the pink ladies working the information desk, where the room of Alex is.

You can hear their shoes on the tile floors as they briskly trek to the surgical intensive care unit. They press the button to open the doors. One of the double doors opens, allowing them passage. They quietly walk to the nurse's station.

"Hello. We are here to see Alex…." Seth's words are interrupted when he hears the voice of Nick.

"You came!" Nick voices, upon seeing the Thompsons, when he and his parents round the corner of a hallway.

Nicole rushes into the arms of Nick.

"I'm so sorry this has happened," Nicole whispers into Nick's ear.

Nick tightly closes his eyes while he embraces Nicole. Their hug generates comfort.

"Hello." Seth reaches to shake the hand of Paul. "It is nice to see you again."

"Yes. We were looking forward to a big family meal today, but this happened." Paul firmly shakes the hand of Seth.

"Yeah, no need to explain. We are certainly thankful to have met Alex early on this summer. We value meeting all of you…as a tremendous blessing," Seth conveys.

"Let's go to the waiting area," Emily suggests.

The families stroll down the hall. Off to the left is a large area. Comfortable chairs, along with a few recliners, and some tables are arranged in the waiting room. The décor is simple, hosting soft neutral colors. The wall décor speaks a theme of nature and promotes a peaceful environment. The families sit down.

"How is Alex? Do you know what happened?" Seth inquires.

Paul nods. "Yes. Alex was on his way home from work. A car in the eastbound lane crossed the median into the westbound lane. The car was weaving out of control. Alex swerved to avoid the car, but unfortunately, his truck clipped it anyway. The impact sent the other vehicle spinning into the median, and sent Alex's truck over the edge of the shoulder, causing it to flip."

The expressions on the family members can write paragraphs.

"What about the other driver?" Laurie questions.

"Well, I went to check if we knew who it was and the driver's status. Apparently, she was headed home from a military base to her parents, when she went into labor…." Paul pauses. "While she was driving!"

"Oh my! Did she and her baby survive?" Laurie asks.

"Yes. Miraculously…they both survived and are expected to make a full recovery," Emily informs.

"Have you visited her yet?" Nicole asks.

"No. I will though. Just to make sure she and her baby are alright," Nick discloses.

"I think that is a good idea. I can join you since I am here today," Nicole offers.

Nick smiles. "Yes. I like that even better."

Paul leans over and rests his forearms on his thighs. He slightly shakes his head. "No one was at fault. The young woman went into early labor. She was not due for three weeks. She was on her way to live with her parents. Her husband was recently killed while on tour, overseas."

The hearts of both families sink upon hearing the information Paul discloses.

"And we do not know about Alex. His parents and brother are in with him right now." Paul sighs.

Emily reaches her arm around Paul and caresses the back of her husband with her hand.

Silence, coupled with sorrow, ladens the room.

After some time, Nick stands. He peers into the eyes of each parent and then focuses on Nicole. "As you all know, I spoke with you about marrying Nicole."

Nicole perks up and eagerly listens.

Nick outlines, "I want to give my life to loving her, protecting her, providing for her, and simply able to date her…every day of every year."

Smiles appear on the faces of the families. You can feel positive energy recharging everyone's spirits. Seth and Laurie stand.

Laurie reaches to hug Nick. "You have my blessing!"

Seth also steps next to Nick to give an approving hug. "I could not have picked out a better man for my daughter. As I told you a few weeks back, you have my blessing!"

Paul and Emily stand, along with Nicole. Everyone exchanges hugs.

"I have not heard a 'yes'." Paul grins.

"I haven't heard a proposal." Nicole glows. She expresses playfulness.

"Well, this was not my plan today. I mean, it was my plan, but this accident happened so…the ring is at home…." Nick lowers himself onto one knee in front of Nicole and gently takes her hand into his hands and cradles her hand between his hands. He gazes into her blue eyes. "Nicole Elizabeth Thompson, it would honor me, if you will have me as your husband, so I can have the opportunity to love you and make good on my words every day of our lives. Will you marry me?"

Nicole lights up! The parents stand next to each other. Laurie's hands are folded in prayer. Emily and Paul have an arm around each other. Seth's arm is around his wife.

"I will! Nicolas Charles Parks! I am honored to be Mrs. Parks!" Nicole hops up and down. Nick stands and leads Nicole into his arms. They exchange a loving kiss.

Nicole slightly pulls her head back to gaze into the eyes of Nick. "I can hear your words though none are spoken."

Nick smiles. "When I look in your eyes, I can hear you without any words spoken."

"I love you!" Nicole declares.

"I love you!" Nick confirms.

There is conversation in the room. They keep the volume of their voices low, being mindful they are in the surgical ICU waiting area.

Brief discussions on topics in regards to when Nick will join Nicole on campus, when they will be married, where they will live, are interrupted when Alex's parents, Jack and Vickie, enter the room, along with Aaron, Alex's younger brother.

Paul extends his hand to shake Jack's hand.

"The doctor came in, and he believes Alex will have a full recovery. He said it's a miracle that he does not have a head trauma or broken bones," Jack summarizes.

"That's great news!" Paul nods at Jack and pats his arm.

"What are his injuries?" Seth asks.

"Other than some deep bruising, his bladder ruptured, which they promptly repaired. They are going to keep him a few days. The doctor and surgeon repeatedly conveyed to us that it is a miracle he is alive," Jack summarizes. "...and without any broken bones or head trauma!"

The other parents express the same sentiments of what magnificent news it is.

Nick reaches for Nicole's hand. "Alex is going to be my...well our...best man."

Vickie places her hands over her mouth then extends her arms outward to the couple. "That is beautiful news! He was thrilled when he told us you asked him to be your best man!"

Nick and Nicole hug Vickie.

Jack grins. "Seeing the two of you should brighten up his spirit."

"Aaron, will you be our groomsman?" Nick requests.

Aaron smiles and nods. "I would love that. Thank you."

"Well, if you all will excuse us...." Nick adds.

Emily and Laurie simultaneously express, "Yes. Be on your way."

CHAPTER 6

Meeting the Other Driver

Nick and Nicole stroll the aisles.

"I don't know that anyone will tell us where she is," Nick whispers.

"I know." Nicole curls her lips.

"I could find a phone and call Doug." Nick thinks aloud.

"You know what? I bet maybe she is on the maternity floor." Nicole guesses.

"Yeah, that makes sense," Nick replies.

The couple read the wall plaque to locate where the maternity ward is.

"Well, we can try." Nick leads.

Nicole gently squeezes Nick's hand. "Oh, let's go to the gift shop and buy a present for her and her baby."

"That is very thoughtful." Nick gazes into the eyes of Nicole.

The two remember the gift shop is near the front doors. They navigate their way to the gift shop. After browsing, they decide to purchase a beautiful cross, accompanied with a book of prayers, and a package of two cute generic one-piece pajamas.

"Oh! We should buy her some flowers!" Nicole exclaims.

"We should." Nick winks.

The couple leave the hospital gift shop with a cute sack containing the gifts and a bouquet of flowers. Nick and Nicole step into the elevator and select floor three. They smile at each other.

"After this, let's go see Alex," Nick suggests.

"Yes!" Nicole agrees.

The elevator doors open. They exit the elevator and look up and down the hall to determine which way to go.

"Oh! There's a sign!" Nicole points.

Nick slightly tilts his head to the side and inhales a deep breath, then releases it. "Do you think this is a good idea?" Apprehension creeps into Nick.

"Yes. She probably feels sick that she caused the crash. She probably wonders if Alex is alive, even though she does not know his name," Nicole assures.

Nick nods.

The two arrive at the maternity ward and enter through the double doors. They approach the nurse at the desk.

"Hi. How may I help you? Oh, what beautiful flowers," the nurse at the desk comments.

"Hi! We are looking for the lady that was brought in last night who was involved in a car crash. To my knowledge, she was in labor," Nicole discloses.

"I see. How are you related?" questions the nurse.

Nick and Nicole frown.

"We are not related. I am best friends with the other driver in the accident," Nick explains.

"We were hoping to meet her and tell her our friend will be alright. Maybe that will put her mind she at ease and she can focus her attention to her newborn," Nicole chimes in.

"I see." The nurse tightens the corners of her lips. "Let me ask her if she is feeling up to having visitors."

Nick and Nicole both smile.

"Thank you so much!" Nicole nods.

Nick and Nicole keep a steady eye to see which room the nurse enters. After a short time, the nurse returns and stands in front of them. "She is scared and doesn't want any visitors."

"Oh, please. Here…." Nicole hands the nurse the bag of gifts and reaches for the bouquet of flowers from the hands of Nick. Nicole then hands the flowers to the nurse. "Here. Take these to her. Tell her all will be well. We beg you," Nicole pleads.

The nurse slightly tilts her head. "Alright. I will see what I can do." The nurse carries the bouquet and bag of thoughtful gifts down the hall and into the patient's room.

Nick and Nicole stare at each other.

The nurse steps into the hall. "You two, come on. She will see you."

Nick and Nicole glance at each other, then quickly make their way down the hall.

"Be mindful. She appears to be very fragile right now, emotionally," the nurse whispers.

Nick and Nicole nod.

They enter the room and notice a lovely young woman, most likely, not much older, maybe four to six years older than either of them. Her dark hair is a mess. Her brown eyes appear to be full of tears.

"Hi, my name is Nicole Thompson, and this is my fiancé, Nick Parks." Nicole steps slowly toward the young woman and extends her hand to shake.

The young woman slightly smiles and extends her hand to shake Nicole's hand. "Thank you for the gifts! So very thoughtful of you. My name is Amy Chambers," Amy introduces herself. "Who are you?"

Nick steps forward, though he feels reluctance. "The driver of the other vehicle is my best friend. We grew up together. He is going to be my best man, our best man." Nick smiles and glances at Nicole.

Amy studies the two of them. "How is he?"

Nick tightens his lips. "The surgeon told his family earlier today that he expects Alex to have a full recovery. What about you? Are you alright? How is your baby?"

At that moment, a nurse carries Amy's baby boy into the room.

Nick and Nicole step aside allowing the nurse plenty of room to place the bundle into the arms of Amy.

Amy smiles from ear to ear seeing her little prince.

"I'll give you some time. I will return in say…thirty minutes," the nurse informs.

"Thank you." Amy gently rocks her baby and kisses his forehead. "Now what am I going to name you little one?" Amy then looks up and smiles at Nick and Nicole. "I would introduce you to my little guy…but I haven't come up with his full name."

At that very moment an idea comes to Amy. "What did you say your friend's name is?"

"Alex…well, his legal name is Alexander Jackson Monroe," Nick discloses.

Amy's face lights up. "I would like you to meet my son, Patrick Alexander Chambers."

Nick and Nicole exchange a huge smile.

"Wow! That is so thoughtful of you!" Nick expresses.

"Well, now…there is a full meaning to his name. Patrick is the name of my late husband. He was recently killed in a battle. He was in the army. He and his men were on a mission that went south." Amy inhales a deep breath and slowly exhales. "So, this little guy is Patrick, in honor of his father…who is a hero and a warrior." Amy pauses and lovingly smiles at her precious newborn. "And his middle name shall be Alexander, representing life. I believe if your friend's vehicle would not have clipped mine, I would have been the one going off the shoulder and flipping. I believe with my whole heart that your friend inadvertently saved our lives. His truck clipping me sent me spinning safely into the median. It was very scary. The pains of labor were so powerful I began swerving. I know

I crossed the median and into his way. I am thankful he survived. I hope he will forgive me…I hope to meet him. Please tell him I named my son's middle name after him," Amy details.

Nicole reaches for the hand of Amy and gently, but firmly squeezes it. "We will. And for what it's worth, we appreciate your husband's service to our country."

"Yes. His service is admirable," Nick offers, then shifts his eyes to Nicole. "Speaking of Alex, we need to go see if he can have more visitors yet," Nick comments. He then casts his eyes upon Amy and the baby. "It is very nice to meet you and Patrick. All the best to you."

Amy smiles. "Thank you both so much! You two make a handsome couple. I can tell you share a powerful love."

Nick and Nicole glance at each other and smile, then peer at Amy.

"Thank you. We will come visit again before you are discharged," Nicole states.

"Do you know when that will be?" Nick asks.

"They told me five days. Since Patrick was three weeks early, and they delivered him by cesarean, so, five days is what they say," Amy recalls.

"Alright. Well, we will come back to visit you, Amy Chambers!" Nicole declares.

"I look forward to it!" Amy voices.

Nick and Nicole both nod.

"Oh! Thank you, again, for the thoughtful gifts! They are perfect!" Amy elevates her voice, since Nick and Nicole are at the door.

Nick looks back, "It was our pleasure."

"Oh! I leave for college tomorrow, so I may not see you before you are discharged. Please write down your address and phone number so we can keep in contact." Nicole steps back to Amy. Nicole reaches in her purse for a pen and paper and hands it to Amy.

Amy writes down her parent's address and phone number. "Okay, here you go. I look forward to hearing from you." Amy hands Nicole the paper and pen back.

Nick places one arm around Nicole. She wraps her arm around him and they depart from the maternity ward and return to surgical ICU.

Nick and Nicole stop at the nurse's station.

"May we see Alex now?" Nick questions.

The nurse nods. "Yes, he has been asking for you."

Nick and Nicole enter Alex's room.

Alex lights up.

"Man, it's great to see you awake!" Nick steps over to carefully hug his friend.

"Do you remember what happened?" Nicole asks.

"I do now. I was driving home from work, just crossed the bridge over the river when I saw a car crossing the median and swerving into my lane. It was coming at me head on. I tried to get out of the way. We were going highway speed. I slowed down and swerved to miss the car, but somehow, we still collided. I clipped the car which sent it spinning into the median and I went over the shoulder," Alex recounts.

"Yeah, I know. My dad and I were there." Nick slightly lowers his head.

"I'm sorry to scare you. The surgeon says I am going to be good as new!" Alex voices. "Wait, have you been here since the wreck?"

"Yes. I rode with you in the ambulance," Nick informs.

"You did? Wow, I do not remember. Did you come home from college to see me?" Alex asks Nicole.

Nicole and Nick glance at each other and then return their eyes to Alex.

"No. I leave tomorrow for college," Nicole shares.

"Oh. I thought that was last week," Alex comments. "I must have my days confused." Alex reaches to scratch his cheek. "I thought for sure I have been in here a week."

"No. No, it only happened last night," Nick conveys.

"No way. Man…it sure seems like a week." Alex leans his head back on his pillow and closes his eyes.

"Hey, we are gonna let you sleep. I will see you in a while." Nick places his hand on Alex's forearm and leans to kiss his forehead.

Nicole steps next to Alex and smiles. Alex opens his eyes. "There's that pretty girl that captured the heart of my best friend." Alex smiles. He attempts to keep his eyes open.

Nicole leans in to kiss Alex on his cheek. "You get better. I leave for college tomorrow and I want my best man to get well soon…you hear?" Nicole gently caresses the arm of Alex.

A large grin plasters across the face of Alex. "Yes. I am going to be the best man at your wedding…because I AM the best man! Alex out." Alex drifts off to sleep from the pain cocktail the nurse recently gave him.

Nicole and Nick engage in a quick conversation before they enter the waiting room where their families are.

"I think he may have some memory issues," Nick expresses concern.

"Yes. Understandably so. I'm sure it will go away as the swelling goes down, and as time passes. He may not have trauma, but I imagine there is some swelling. Our bodies have a unique way of healing themselves. Plus of course, the power of prayer." Nicole comforts Nick.

Nick nods.

"Well, this is not my idea of how I wanted to spend our last day together." Nick positions himself in front of Nicole, takes her hands into his hands, and leans his forehead onto her forehead.

"I will see you soon! We have a wedding to plan! I will look for housing for us. I love our life and look forward to every day with you!" Nicole eagerly voices. "Oh… and so you know…." She pulls her forehead from Nick's forehead and peers into his eyes. "I can read your eyes as you can read mine. When I hear your voice, it is like music to my ears…your words ground me and keep my feet steady. My spirit softens in your presence, my heart opens…I smile…knowing YOU-are the loving force-behind everything…that brings peace to my soul." She then places her lips upon Nick's lips.

Their bodies mesh into an embrace of a powerful departure hug.

"Those could be vows," Nick whispers.

"I was thinking toasting words. Our priest will most likely not allow handwritten vows." Nicole giggles.

Nick grins. "Yeah, probably not."

"I just want you to know how I feel, in case something happens to me. I want you to always know what an impact you have on me!" Nicole asseverates.

"Nothing is going to happen to you. But I appreciate your kind words," Nick maintains.

"Oh, we didn't tell Alex about the driver or the baby," Nicole mentions.

"I know. It just did not seem like the right time. I will tell him tomorrow," Nick conveys.

Nicole nods. "Alright. Well, let's go visit with our families."

"Sounds good. You guys should probably get on the road soon. You have a long drive ahead of you tomorrow," Nick comments.

"Not that long, but you are right, we should probably head home. I don't want to leave you. I don't have to go to college. I want to be your wife…now." Nicole gets misty.

Nick leads her into his arms. "I know. We will be married soon."

"I am saving myself for you," Nicole whispers.

"I am saving myself for you," Nick voices. "I will be joining you soon. Maybe in a couple weeks I can come up and we will look for housing together."

"Or I drop out or transfer to a local college. I don't need this. I don't want to be away from you anymore! Ugh! Long distance sucks!" Nicole sternly states.

"Nicole, we are engaged. I'm not going anywhere. This accident has put a hiccup in timing. You want your degree...." Nick's words are interrupted.

"NO. I don't care about a degree! I can go to a local college when the timing is right. All I want, is to be, Mrs. Nicolas Charles Parks. I want to wake to you every day. I want to fall asleep in your arms. I hunger to be with you and begin our life together," Nicole adamantly voices. "You're my guy. I wanna get married as soon as Alex can be our best man!"

"I sure like the sound of all that." Nick kisses Nicole's lips. "Mmm. I feel the same. But, at least go with your parents to the campus tomorrow. Your friend Cami is going to be there, right?"

Nicole nods.

"See...you will be alright. I will be there shortly. And we can get married whatever date you want." Nick comforts Nicole and smiles with love.

"You're right. Okay. September or October? That's when I want to get married," Nicole discloses.

"How about October? We need to give our parents time to invite the people they want. It's already August," Nick states.

"The only person I need at our wedding is you," Nicole charmingly voices.

"You're pretty sweet, ya know?" Nick smiles.

"I didn't realize me leaving for college tomorrow was going to cause me to become so unglued," Nicole shares.

Nick once again leads Nicole into his embrace and lovingly speaks, "I think the trauma of Alex's accident, coupled with you leaving, well, it is just overwhelming for all of us."

Nicole sniffles. "I believe you are right. All of it has thrown me off, though I don't see you being misty."

Nick slightly laughs. "I can tell you, if you saw my heart, you would see it is underwater," Nick confides.

Nicole perks up. "Really?"

"Well, yeah. I don't want you to go. Everything you said, I feel the same way. If I don't have tears, maybe they are all gone from crying and praying so much last night. You and your family coming here today brought sunshine to my heart. But inside, I am a mess. I don't want you to go. It is only temporary. We will be alright and stronger," Nick comforts. "How about our wedding be on October 21st?"

"I LOVE that!" Nicole smiles and basks in his embrace.

Nick's voice calms her. His words make sense.

Chapter 7

Campus Life

Nicole and her parents set out for the college. Nicole drives her car. Her parents follow her in their truck. Cami is already settled into their duplex on campus. Nicole arrives with her parents Sunday afternoon.

"Yea! You are here!" Cami runs to greet Nicole. "Hello, Mr. and Mrs. Thompson!"

"Hello, Cami," Lauric voiccs.

Everyone pitches in to unload and carry luggage and items from the vehicles into their duplex.

"Well, we made short work of that!" Seth nods. "Hey, your mother and I have something for you."

Nicole's eyes light up. "You do not need to get me anything. Your love is all I need."

"Oh, I think your gonna like this." Laurie smiles at her daughter. "Let's go sit down.

They enter the living room and sit on the long green sofa.

Seth hands his daughter a wrapped box. "Here, your mother and I want you to have this."

Nicole excitedly opens the box. "What? A phone? How cool is this!" Nicole squeezes both of her parents. "Oh, my gosh! I can't wait to call Nick. Wait! He doesn't have a cell phone. I will call his house number. Will that work?"

"Yes, honey, you can call anywhere. Don't worry, Nick was gifted a cell phone from his parents today as well. We already programmed his number and our numbers into it," Seth informs.

"What? You guys bought cell phones, too?" Nicole is stunned and pleasantly surprised.

"Yes. Both of your older sister's phone numbers are in your phone as well. We entered several numbers we thought you may need. You can add more," Laurie details.

"You're right! This present IS a treasure! Wow! Thank you!" Nicole exclaims.

CHAPTER 8

Alex is Discharged

"What a welcome home party this is!" Alex expresses. He is very happy to see his friends at his family home. "And look at you, college girl. How is campus life treating you?" Alex smiles at Nicole.

"It's alright. I am ready to be done and come back! I miss you and Nick!" Nicole hugs Alex.

"You'll be done soon enough. You're wedding to my buddy here, is approaching. That'll be cool!" Alex smiles.

"It will!" Nicole reaches for Nick's hand. "I cannot wait!" Nicole's smile lights up the room. "I am so glad you are going to be our best man, and Cami, our maid of honor! Just perfect!"

"I agree!" Alex smiles. He lowers himself to sit in a comfortable recliner.

Alex's parents, Jack and Vickie, offer a variety of food that spreads out on the island. There is also a creatively decorated double chocolate fudge cake with the words 'Welcome Home Alex' written across the center of the top.

"Help yourselves when y'all are hungry. We have plenty of food," Vickie announces.

The guests glance over at the well displayed variety of meats, cheese, breads, chips, drinks, with the cake as the centerpiece on the island. Paper plates, forks, and napkins are also offered. Guests help themselves to the food throughout the afternoon.

Nick, Nicole, and Cami, surround Alex. The four reminisce on activities they enjoyed during the first two and a half months of summer. They laugh and giggle.

"So, Alex, what are your plans?" Cami sweetly smiles at Alex.

"Well, I have applied to the seminary. I believe God is calling me to be his servant in the vocation of priesthood," Alex shares.

"Wow! So, I guess we are not going to date." Cami giggles.

Alex blushes. "Don't think I have not thought about it, blondie. You are pretty cute, ya know." Alex grins. "And, your personality is undeniably charming, along with solid. It has been a great summer with the four of us hanging. I value my friendships with each of you, but my calling is to serve Christ Jesus."

"I think that is admirable and beautiful!" Nicole exclaims.

Cami slightly blushes and places her hand on Alex's arm and peers into his eyes. "I think that is very wise and noble, to answer a call like that with a 'Yes.' I am so proud of you. We all are!"

Nick and Nicole both nod their heads in agreement.

The evening winds down and the girls are going to drive back to campus. They each make rounds to say their goodbyes.

"Alex, you take care! You are the best man anyone could hope for! I will see you before our wedding!" Nicole hugs Alex.

Alex grins, "Well, I must say, when my buddy met you, it was like two pieces in a puzzle that fit perfectly together."

"Aww! You are the best, Alex. I love you!" Nicole reaches and gives Alex another departure hug.

"Be safe out there." Alex salutes.

"Hey, I'll be back in a minute. "I'm going to see Nicole out," Nick voices to Alex.

Alex nods.

Nick and Nicole stroll hand in hand to her car while Cami finishes saying her goodbyes.

"Mm, not much longer and we will be Mr. and Mrs. Nicolas Parks." Nicole smiles. She glances at Nick.

He wraps his arms around her. "I like the sound of that."

"Hey! Cami insists I go to some party with her next weekend. She has been dying to go, but wants me to go with her. I don't want to go…would you want to come up and go with us?"

Nick notices how important this is to Nicole. Nick quietly confirms, "Yes. I would be honored to attend the party with you and Cami."

Nicole leaps into Nick's arms. "Thank you! Thank you! I know this is not what you or I really like to do…but, thank you! Why God blessed me with a social butterfly as a best friend, I will never know." Nicole giggles.

"Yeah, I hear ya." Nick lovingly smiles. "I like spending time with you no matter where we are."

The two peer into each other's eyes.

"What are your thoughts for our future?" Nick asks Nicole.

Nicole lights up. "Well, getting married October 21st! Then, we move you up to campus. We get our degrees…then I would love to live back near both of our families. I would LOVE to live in the country, near the lake, with a long driveway, lined with autumn maples!"

Nick and Nicole sway in each other's arms while mapping out their plans.

"I like that idea. I think we should begin looking for property before we graduate. Do you want children?" Nick asks.

"Of course! Little Nicks' running around, and maybe a little Nicole or two." Nicole giggles. "Yes, I agree, we should begin looking for property now."

Nick grins. "I like the way you think."

They exchange a kiss. Cami comes out.

"Whenever you're ready." Cami gets in the car.

"I'll be seeing you, my soon-to-be husband." Nicole's eyes sparkle with joy.

"I'll be seeing you, my soon-to-be Mrs." Nick hugs Nicole one last time.

Nicole whispers in his ear, "I like the sound of that. I will see you Saturday!"

"Yes. I love you." Nick reaches for the driver's door and opens it for Nicole. They exchange one more kiss. She gets into the car. Nick closes the door.

Cami and Nicole both wave. Nicole starts her car and puts it drive. Nick waves watching them drive away.

CHAPTER 9

Accompanying Cami

"I think this dress looks cute!" Cami turns around in front of the full-length mirror. "What do you think?"

"I don't know. What is your objective?" Nicole questions.

"Gosh, to wear a dress I feel confident in." Cami stares in the mirror and studies her outfit. "Hmm, I think I will change it." Cami turns to step into the closet and notices Nicole's attire. "Are you gonna wear *that*?"

Nicole steps in front of the mirror and spins. "Yep. I like it."

Cami makes a face. "What is *your* statement?"

"Comfort…engaged…leave me alone…." Nicole giggles, "Plus I'm on my period."

"Well, I think you chose well!" Cami giggles. "Okay, what about this dress?"

"Do you feel confident in it?" Nicole asks.

Cami nods. "I do."

"Alright then." Nicole nods.

"When will Nick be here?" Cami anxiously asks. She is looking forward to dancing.

"He should be here in about thirty minutes," Nicole reminds.

"Oh, I guess we did get ready early." Cami giggles.

"Yeah, we did." Nicole dances around the house and tidies up their place.

The girls hear a phone ringing. They exchange an inquisitive expression.

"Oh! I think that must be your cell phone!" Cami expresses with excitement.

Nicole runs to the room where the phone is on charge. "Hello?"

"Hey, babe." Nick addresses.

"Hello! We were just wondering about you." Nicole lights up hearing Nick's voice.

"Hey, I am going to be a little late. There was a truck hauling some construction materials…anyway, some debris flew out of his truck. I swerved to miss it, but still ended up running over a nail. Of course, my tire blew. So, I am on the shoulder and am going to change it," Nick details.

"Oh my! I am thankful you are not hurt!" Nicole conveys.

"Thanks! Me too. If you girls want to go ahead, I will join you as soon as I get up and running." Nick opens the trunk of his car.

"I guess we can go." Nicole glances at Cami and observes how eager she is. "Alright, Nick, we will go ahead. You be safe. See you in a bit." Nicole reaches for the hand of Cami.

"Yes. You two be safe. I will be there shortly." Nick taps a button on his phone to end the call. He sets the phone down in his front seat, then returns to his trunk to remove the jack and spare tire.

"Okay, let's go!" Cami grabs her purse from the chair and slings it over one shoulder crossing to the other side.

Nicole declares, "This cell phone almost won't fit in my purse."

The girls giggle and leave their duplex. They stroll across campus to a party Cami has been wanting to attend.

"We should have rules," Nicole suggests.

"Rules? Like what?" Cami asks.

"Rules like we do not leave each other's sight. Also, when one is ready to leave, we both leave," Nicole suggests.

"Great…since you don't even want to go, we will be leaving upon arrival," Cami jests, though serves it with a dash of truth.

"That's true, however, I know this is important to you. So, I will stay as long as I can take it. Plus, Nick will be here soon, so that will be fun," Nicole assures.

"Yeah," Cami comments, as they continue walk. "When do you think he will move here?"

"Not sure. Alex's wreck put things on hold," Nicole explains. "Well, definitely not until after our wedding. I think that is the plan, then he will begin second semester."

"Yeah…that was scary!" Cami points. "We are almost there."

Nicole peers across the street and down the block and sighs. "There is a LOT of people.

"Yeah! It should be fun!" Cami grabs Nicole's hand and leads the way.

Stewart, an athlete, who has been attempting to get Nicole's attention in calculus class ever since he met her, comes up behind Cami and Nicole. "What can I get you two lovely ladies to drink?"

Cami lights up. "Gosh, I don't know. Maybe a beer?"

Nicole discreetly reaches her hand to tug at Cami's dress and whispers, "We are not legally old enough."

"So, what will it be ladies? Stewart questions again.

"Ya know, I am not really a drinker…I'm good. Nothing, thank you," Nicole firmly states.

Cami looks up at Stewart, "I'll have a beer."

"What kind?" Stewart questions.

Cami and Nicole glance at each other inquisitively.

"In a bottle?" Cami declares.

Stewart grins. He knows they are naïve. "Come on, let me get you something." He shifts his eyes to Nicole.

"Lemonade?" Nicole questions.

"I'm pretty sure they have some. I'll be right back." Stewart quickly struts to the large bar.

"He seems nice," Cami comments.

"I guess. But I am NOT interested! I wonder where Nick is. He should be here by now." Nicole glances around. "I am engaged and my entire heart and body are for Nick," Nicole resounds. "Maybe I should go out to the road and see if he got lost."

"No, you can't leave me. You must make sure I am safe. You promised," Cami convinces. "You came up with the rules. And besides…he is NOT going to get lost! This party is so loud, and large…you can't miss it!" Cami assures.

Nicole nods. "You're right. We need to protect each other. I will be here for you!"

"Come on…answer your phone," Nick voices aloud. *I cannot believe there is one lane for all these miles on the turnpike!* Nick glances at his speedometer. *Down to forty miles per hour.* Nick redials Nicole's number. "Hey babe, it is one lane for miles, so I will be a little longer. I am sorry. I left in time, but not in time for delays. See you soon! I love you!" Nick ends his call after he leaves Nicole a message.

Stewart orders the drinks. He covertly pulls out something from his pocket and drops it into the glass of lemonade. Stewart then motions for his friend, Martin. Martin works his way through the crowd. "What's up?"

"Hey, you see those two girls over there? Will you get the blonde to dance with you?" Stewart requests.

"Sure, why?" Martin inquires.

"They are inseparable, and I want to visit with the brunette," Stewart lies.

"Sure, buddy. She's cute. I will have no problem dancing with her." Martin smiles and pats Stewart on the back.

Stewart and Martin approach the girls. Stewart hands Cami a beer. "Cami, this is my friend, Martin."

Martin smiles. "Hello. Would you like to dance?"

Cami glances at Nicole.

"Hey, we will be right here, waiting," Stewart assures, though he deceives. "Oh, I almost forgot, here is your lemonade." Stewart hands Nicole the glass of lemonade.

"Thank you." Nicole takes the glass. "Cami, if you want to dance, I'll wait right here."

"We could dance," Stewart suggests.

"No, thank you. I am engaged. Remember?" Nicole's forehead forms creases.

"I don't see what one dance will hurt," Stewart attempts to be persuasive.

"To me…it will," Nicole remains adamant.

"Okay, I'm gonna dance with Martin." Cami reaches to squeeze Nicole's hand. Cami tags a gulp of the beer and sets it on the table.

Nicole smiles at Cami. "Yes, enjoy yourself."

Martin takes a hand of Cami's and leads her to the crowded dance floor. They enjoy the up-beat dance music.

Nicole does not hear her phone ringing in her purse. She takes a swallow of the lemonade. Stewart keenly pays attention. Nicole takes another drink and sighs.

Nice party. I like seeing Cami have fun. I am ready to go but I will stay for Cami. Nicole thinks to herself.

"Yeah know, maybe in another life you would dance with me," Stewart suggests.

Nicole feels woozy. Stewart's words sound garbled. She begins to collapse; however, Stewart immediately catches her and lifts her into his arms. He tries to hide his grin. He turns, and without bringing attention to himself, carries Nicole up the stairs.

Cami and Martin dance back to their table.

"I wonder where Nicole went." Cami scans around.

"Probably to the bathroom. Stewart may be showing her where it is. There are several," Martin responds.

Cami finishes her beer and orders another one. Martin and Cami go back to the dance floor after Cami slams another beer. Martin and Cami enjoy dancing together.

Nick leaves his phone in his car. He treks onto the grounds of the large party. There are so many people indoors and out. He strolls through the crowd in hopes to find Nicole. People ask him if he wants a drink, girls ask him to dance, he feels out of his element, though he is polite to everyone. He finally spies Cami on the dance floor. Nick stands off to the side waiting for an opportunity to get Cami's attention.

"Oh, do you mind? I see a friend that I need to say hello to," Cami speaks loudly into Martin's ear.

"Sure. I'll catch up with you later," Martin conveys.

Cami dance steps her way across the dance floor to Nick. "Hey there! Man, Nicole is going to be so happy to see you!"

"Yeah. Where is she?" Nick asks.

A look of concern crosses the face of Cami. She scans the entire area. "Wow. I don't see her anywhere. I bet she went home."

"Without you? Don't you guys have some girl code?" Nick inquires.

"We do…let's see…Martin came and asked me to dance. Stewart brought Nicole a lemonade…hmm…I do not see either of them. I bet she went back to our place," Cami assures.

"Who is Stewart?" Nick questions.

"Ah, he is nobody. A jock who met Nicole in calculus. He annoys her. She made it clear to him she is NOT interested and that she is engaged. Oh Nick, she is going to be so happy you finally made it!" Cami details.

Nick exhales and feels a little better. "Alright, I will go to your duplex. She sent me the address. I tried calling her, but I can see why she didn't answer. She probably did not hear it ring."

"That's my guess. Okay, I'll see you there later," Cami states.

"Don't you think you should go home now? It seems you have been drinking. Let me take you home," Nick gently persuades.

Cami nods. "I think you're right. Take me home, Nick!" Cami raises one arm in the air and shouts out, "Woohoo! Best dancing ever!" She then slightly falls into Nick's shoulder.

He locks arms at their elbows to securely escort Cami to his car.

Nick assists Cami into the duplex and to her bedroom. Cami falls back onto her bed. Nick lifts her feet and legs and gently makes sure her entire body is in the bed. He takes off her shoes and covers her with a blanket, then leaves her room and closes the door.

Nick does not understand why Nicole is not yet home. He is concerned. Nick does not even know where to begin to look. He decides to go back to the party and search. Nick treks his way across the campus to the location of the party. He makes his way through the crowd of partying kids. He pulls out his wallet. He removes a picture of Nicole and begins to question random people, "Have you seen this girl?" The reply is the same. "No." This continues for quite some time as he combs through crowd of college students. Finally, Nick makes his way inside and approaches almost everyone. He realizes most of them have been drinking. Some mention they think they have her in a class. Nick decides to walk to the bar and question the bartender. "Have you seen this girl tonight?"

The bartender studies the picture and peers at Nick. "Yeah. Hours ago. She was with another girl…a blonde. Haven't seen them for hours."

Nicole rolls over. She feels groggy. *I feel like I have a hangover, though I have never had one. Where AM I?* the light from the city acts as a nightlight. She feels her skin. *Where are my clothes?* Nicole reaches for a lamp that is sitting on a table next to the bed she is lying in. She flips on the light, squints her eyes, and tries to figure out WHERE on earth she is. She spies her clothes thrown across the floor. *Why would I throw my clothes? Oh, ouch!* She grabs her forehead and lies back onto the pillow. *My head! What is wet in the bed?* As she continues to become alert, she sits up and turns to place her feet on the floor. She doubles over experiencing painful cramping. *What is wrong with me?* She stands and turns to look what is wet on the bed. *Did I spill water?* She pulls back the cover and sees blood! *That's right…I remember…I am on my period. Where am I? Why am I naked?* Nicole begins to panic. She frantically picks up each article of clothing and gets dressed. Just then, she hears what sounds like a shower door close. *Oh, my God, help me!* A large of array of thoughts race through her mind.

Stewart steps out of the bathroom in a towel wrapped around his waist. "Well, look who's awake." He walks over to kiss her cheek.

Nicole ducks to ward off his attempt.

"You were one ***SWEEET*** cherry! Mm, mm!" Stewart boasts.

"What?" Nicole is shaken, as is her voice.

"I wanted to be the first to have you." Stewart raises his shoulders, bends his arms at his elbows, and holds his arms out with his palms up. "And…mm…mm…are you sweet!"

"What?!" Nicole cries hysterically. "You robbed me? I have been saving myself for my fiancé! You piece of all things bad! How could you do this to me! You drugged me? How could you!"

Stewart smiles with cockiness. "You know you'll be back! I am sure looking forward to having you again!"

"Back? I don't even remember! I HATE YOU! Why did you do this to me? Why did you rob me!" Nicole screams! She reaches for books on shelves and begins throwing them across his room.

"Hey! You need to calm down." Stewart attempts to catch the books being hurled.

"Calm down? You stole from me! You robbed me!" Nicole shouts.

There is a loud pounding at the door. Stewart steps to the door and opens it.

"Is there a problem?" One of the campus security officers' questions.

"No, just a lover's spat," Stewart maintains, then he lowers his voice and quietly says, "Her period started and she's just a little nuts, thinking I want someone else."

The officer scans the room and sees a significant amount of blood on the sheets. "Are you alright, Miss?"

Nicole won't show her face. She barely nods.

"Thank you for checking. It's nice to know you are a book throw away," Stewart charms.

"Anytime." The campus security team leaves.

"Now, we have been seen as a couple," Stewart announces.

"We…are NOT…A COUPLE!" Nicole articulates her words with utter loathing and directness. Nicole gathers her things, rushes to the door, and leaves. She decides to slip into the fire escape stairwell next to his door. She swiftly descends the stairs undetected. She dashes out into the early morning air. The sun has not yet risen, and all is quiet on the streets. Nicole runs as fast as she can as many blocks as she can away from that place!

Stewart scans the room and shakes his head at the sheets he must wash and the clean-up before him. He thinks to himself, *all in a night well spent.*

Nick notices a staircase. He decides to investigate. He runs up the stairs leaping steps by twos and threes. He checks the doors he sees. The doors are either locked, or a bathroom, or a janitorial closet. He spies campus security officers coming from the end of the hall. From years of observing his dad handle emergency situations, his knowledge comes into play.

"Hello, officers. Everything alright down there?" Nick questions.

"Yeah, sorry to disturb you. Just a lover's quarrel," one of the officers mentions.

"I guess that happens." Nick politely gestures.

The officers tip their heads as they pass Nick and descend the staircase.

Nick looks up and down the dismal hallway. *I guess I will head back to the duplex. Maybe Nicole is back there.* Nick darts down the stairs and notices the crowd is thinning. Nick decides to search around the area again before he navigates his way back to the duplex.

Nicole feels shame, outrage, hate, hurt, and all things accompanied with being robbed of such a valuable gift of herself; her treasure, that she was saving for Nick.

I need to clean up. I need to see a doctor. I need to see a priest. I wish I was dead. Many thoughts flood Nicole. She sees the steeple of a Catholic Church on her way home. Nicole decides to go there first. She climbs the church steps. The door is still locked. Nicole sits on the top step with her knees pulled to her chest. She leans against the corner of the wall near the entrance and closes her eyes Nicole feels sick. She feels numb.

"Dear. My dear…." A nun leans over and gently nudges Nicole.

Nicole opens her eyes and looks up.

"Hello, my dear. My name is Sister Agnes. Are you alright?" The nun gently smiles.

Nicole places her hands on the stone wall of the church and pushes herself to stand. She immediately grabs her abdomen.

Sister Agnes notices blood trickling down Nicole's legs. "Come with me, child."

Sister Agnes places her arm around Nicole and leads her to the convent beside the church. They enter. Upon entry, other sisters flock to Sister Agnes and Nicole.

"I found her on the church steps. Sister Catherine, will you please show her to the shower? And Sister Catherine, will you please get some clothes for her? What is your name, my dear?" Sister Agnes directs orders and asks.

"Nicole. Nicole Thompson." Nicole glances around.

"It is nice to meet you, Nicole. You came to the right place. We will get you to a doctor as soon as you clean up," Sister Agnes informs.

While Nicole is showering, Sister Catherine whispers to Sister Agnes, "Are you not worried she will wash away evidence?"

"No. All will be well," Sister Agnes assures.

The shower water cascading over Nicole calms her. She tries not to think about anything. Nicole turns off the water reaches for a towel, dries, and steps out of the shower. She spies clean clothes, and everything she needs. Nicole inhales and exhales, feeling secure in the protection of the nun's love. She dresses, brushes her teeth, and does not even want to mess with her hair. Nicole again inhales a deep breath. She exhales, and then exits the bathroom.

"Here, have some water," Sister Agnes offers. She also sets a bowl of fruit in front of Nicole.

"Thank you." Nicole nods. Nicole drinks some water and eats some fresh berries. "Thank you. This is perfect." Nicole wipes her lips.

"You are welcome. Are you ready?" Sister Agnes asks.

Nicole nods and scoots her chair back, stands, and pushes her chair under the table.

Sister Agnes leads Nicole to the car the parish owns. "I'll drive you to the doctor."

Nicole nods. "Thank you, so very much, Sister."

They reach the office and enter the closet location opened on Sunday's. The nurse quickly takes Nicole to the exam room while Sister Agnes waits.

The doctor takes some samples for lab tests. "I am sorry if I have caused you any discomfort." Doctor Valorie Sims hands the nurse tissue samples.

Nicole inhales a deep breath. "It's okay."

"You may experience some pain for several days," Doctor Sims conveys.

Nicole nods her head. "I understand."

"I will send these labs out to be tested. I will have a nurse contact you with the results as soon have we receive them," Doctor Sims informs.

"Thank you," Nicole quietly voices.

"Honey, I am going to give you a list of counselors to speak to about this. I recommend you talk to someone," Doctor Sims encourages.

"Thank you." Nicole answers, though she has no intention of speaking of this ever again, to anyone.

"Nicole, one more thing," Doctor Sims voices.

Nicole looks over at the doctor.

"I urge you to report this," Doctor Sims insists.

Nicole leaves the exam room and approaches Sister Agnes. Sister Agnes wraps her arm around Nicole and leads her to the car. "My child, God led you to us," Sister Agnes voices.

Nicole looks over at Sister Agnes, gazes into her beautiful eyes, and smiles. "I know. I was walking home when I noticed the steeple. I was led to you. Thank you, Sister Agnes, for taking care of me."

"You are welcome. Where do you live? I will drive you home." Sister Agnes comes to a stop at the stoplight.

"On Lark Lane. It's on campus." Nicole points.

"Yes. I know where that is." Sister Agnes drives navigating the turns until she reaches Lark Lane.

Nick has been awake all night searching for Nicole. Exhausted, he now waits by his car.

Cami steps outside and squints her eyes from the morning sun. "Is Nicole out here with you?" Cami scans around and asks.

"No. I searched for her all night. I think we need to contact her parents," Nick anxiously asserts.

Cami and Nick both hear the rumble of a sports car coming down the road.

"These are nice duplexes. Which duplex is yours?" Sister Agnes asks.

"Yes. They are. My friend, Cami, and I were very fortunate to find one." Nicole scans down the road. "Stop! Now!" Nicoles ducks.

Sister Agnes pulls over. "What is it, dear?"

Nicole panics and begins to cry. "Look down the road. You see that nice sports car? That is my fiancé, Nick with the dark hair, about my height standing a few feet away from his car. My girlfriend, Cami, is on the sidewalk to our place, and the other guy that just arrived is…well…he is the one that did this to me! He is the one that robbed me of my gift to my fiancé! Why won't God just let me die? Why did this happen? I love Nick so much! He is everything to me! I was saving myself for him. This is terrible!" Nicole peeks her head above the dash to view the interaction. "Sister, I am going to get out. Thank you for all your kindness to me. Please tell the other sisters 'Thank you' for me. How can I ever repay you?"

"Oh, Nicole, pray for us." Sister Agnes sweetly smiles at Nicole. "Pray for others. Pray God will always lead you, and be a light of his unwavering love everywhere life takes you. You have great inner strength, whether you see it or not."

Nicole weeps. "But I LOVE Nick! I want to marry him and be his forever."

Sister Agnes squeezes the hand of Nicole. "Know that all things will work out."

Nicole nods.

"Come back and visit the sisters and I," Sister Agnes requests.

"Yes! I will!" Nicole reaches over to give Sister Agnes a hug. Nicole then grabs her things and gets out of the car. She hesitantly walks toward home. She witnesses what looks like words being exchanged.

"Oh, you must be Nicole's fiancé. Whew Wee! She was some fine sweet cherry! That's for sure!" Stewart brags when he steps out of his vehicle.

"What?" Nick is aghast! His expression shifts to that of disgust.

"Oh, yeah," Stewart begins to outline the fabricated details but spies Nicole approaching. "Well, looky there, you can ask her yourself! Guess she just wanted to have a romp with a college man before she married you!" Stewart pokes Nick in the center of his chest. "You know, have some experience...." Stewart conveys with arrogance.

Fires of outrage and hurt burns within Nick. He clenches his left hand and throws a punch directly into the center of Stewart's gut. Stewart doubles over. Nick opens his car door. He glances down the street and sees Nicole carrying her bag. Nick then glares at Cami. "You can tell your friend our wedding is off! Tell her don't bother calling me!" Nick gets into his car, slams the door, backs up, and barrels down the street in the opposite direction.

Nicole takes a few steps and cries out, "Nick! Nick!" Nicole glances back to see if Sister Agnes is still there. She is. Nicole runs as fast as she can to her duplex. By the time she reaches home, Stewart is holding his stomach, but standing upright. Cami remains standing on the sidewalk in shock.

Nicole takes the handle of her bag, grips it tightly and slings it, hitting Stewart on the side of his face. "YOU DID THIS!" Nicole screams!

"Stewart rubs his cheek. "You'll be back. You liked it." Stewart's haughtiness is repulsive.

"LIKED IT?! HELL, I DON'T EVEN REMEMBER IT! DO YOU HAVE TO DRUG ALL THE GIRLS SO SOMEONE WILL HAVE YOU?! Nicole spits on his shoes.

Stewart points at Nicole. "Look, little girl. The campus security has already deemed you as a wild card and has witnessed your violence. I can press charges," Stewart indicates.

"You piece of waste!" Nicole inhales a deep breath and remembers teachings from church. She exhales. "Stewart. I am sorry that I threw your books, also, though I appreciate your interest in me, I really have no interest in anyone now."

"What about my sheets?" Stewart smirks.

"Well, now, that's on you really, isn't it?" Nicole goes numb and suppresses her emotions.

There is silence. The three young adults hear the distinct sound of a car door close. They turn their heads to view down the street at the same time. They see a nun, standing tall, in her Habit.

A smidgen of hope enters Nicole when she sees Sister Agnes.

"Who is that?!" Stewart questions.

"An angel of God that watches over us," Nicole calmly reveals.

"I'm outta here." Stewart rushes to his car.

"Stewart?" Nicole imparts.

"What?" Stewart turns to look at Nicole.

"I pray the best for you." Nicole slightly tilts her head. "Because if you experience the best, maybe you won't feel the need to be a beast."

"Yeah, right." Stewart shakes his head.

"No, for real, right now, Father God, forgive Stewart for his cruel and selfish actions. Grant his heart desire to seek you and your truth. Strengthen his soul and lead his path, that he may find you. In Jesus' Name, we pray. Amen." Nicole drops her folded hands to her side.

Cami whispers, "Amen."

"Who are you!" Stewart scoffs.

"Hopefully the last girl you will be cruel and selfish to!" Nicole folds her arms in front of her.

Stewart shakes his head and gets in his car, closes the door, and drives away.

Nicole views down the road and watches Sister Agnes drop her hands that were folded in prayer, to her side. Sister Agnes waves and gets into her car.

Nicole slightly smiles, nods, and waves.

"Oh, my gosh!" Cami runs to Nicole's side. "I can only imagine what has happened."

Cami and Nicole embrace. They put an arm around each other and walk inside.

"I have a lot to tell you, but first, I am going to call my parents and tell them to come and get me." Nicole releases her arm from around Cami once they step inside. "This isn't for me. Sure, I can continue to attend college here. I am strong enough, but this is a sharp turn from the direction I have been planning for my life. I want to go home. I need to. I'm sure Nick is going to call off the wedding. I am not worthy of him now. I was so looking forward to being each other's first and having that gift for our lives to each other. I honestly don't know where to go from here." Nicole breaks down and weeps.

Cami draws her into her arms. The best friends hug. They both mourn.

"Yeah, Nick did say the wedding is off and not to contact him," Cami whispers, as she firmly holds Nicole.

Nicole nods into Cami's shoulder. "I know. I figured."

"Honey, you have got to tell Nick, or I will." Cami insists. Cami peers into Nicole's eyes.

"NO!" Nicole cries out. "He must not know! For one thing, Nick will be so angry, he will beat Stewart up. Stewart will press charges…Nick does not need that! And NO! Nick cannot know. He will strongly push for *me* to press charges…and I can't! I do not want to go through all the hassle of court and be humiliated in front of everyone! No one must ever know! Promise me, Cami! Promise me!" Nicole pleads.

"Alright. I promise. But it is horrible for you and Nick not to be together over this." Cami feels sorrow.

Nicole sobs. "I know. But I do not want charges pressed against Nick for battery, because I have no doubt he will beat Stewart up. Nor do I want to be hassled with all the court process.

Cami shakes her head. "I understand. This is horrible."

"It is." Nicole weeps.

CHAPTER 10

Ghosted & Haunted

Weeks pass since the incident. Nick spends his time throwing himself into his work and hanging with Alex. Nick has made the decision not to attend college at the university and decides to go to the local college. Sometimes, Alex and Nick visit Amy and her son, Patrick. At the end of each day, Nick writes letters to Nicole, but never finishes them. He is consumed with not knowing WHY she would do this to him, to them. He feels betrayed. Nick feels heartbroken. He misses Nicole. He wonders if he can ever forgive her. Is his love greater than her betrayal?

During these same weeks, Nicole deeply mourns. She is heartbroken and feels robbed of the gift she was saving for Nick for their wedding night. She feels she is of no value. Nicole often lays in bed most hours of each day. Seth and Laurie make attempts to engage with her. Nicole displays no interest in wanting to interact. Nicole deeply misses Nick. She longs to hear his voice, along with the laughter he brings to her. She remembers their unspoken words. She misses everything about him.

Laurie carries in the mail. She notices one addressed to Nicole. The return address is from a laboratory. *She has been waiting for this.* Laurie dashes up the stairs to Nicole's room and knocks. Laurie then lets herself in. "I have something for you, sweetie."

Nicole sits up in her bed.

Laurie sits beside her daughter and hands her the envelope. They exchange eye contact.

Nicole manages to get it open though she is shaky. Nicole reads the results and cries.

Alarmed, Laurie reaches for the letter. She reads it and places her hand on the arm of Nicole. "Oh, honey, this is WONDERFUL news! Praise the Lord you are safe and healthy.

"I know, I have just been praying God would kill me or heal me," Nicole speaks between cries.

"Well, honey, I would say he is going to heal you. This is such wonderful news." Laurie reaches to hug her daughter and holds Nicole very securely. "Life is going to be alright."

Nicole rests in her mother's arms.

"Now, your sisters made it in late last night. Come down for breakfast," Laurie instructs.

Nicole nods. "Alright. I will be right there."

Seth meets Laurie at the stairs. "Everything alright?"

"Yes, I think Nicole just needed another good cry. Her labs all came back healthy," Laurie informs her husband.

"Praise God!" Seth motions for Laurie to join him in the office.

Laurie follows Seth into their home office. Seth turns to face his wife.

"I am still so furious about this! I want to drive up to campus and look for that…that trash!" Seth keeps his voice low.

"I know you do. We have talked about this before. It will do no good," Laurie reaffirms.

"I would feel better," Seth resounds.

"Oh, I am sure you would…unleashing your whuppin' on him," Laurie acknowledges.

"Exactly." Seth paces. He turns back and peers at his wife. "I feel I failed that I could not protect her!"

Laurie steps next to Seth and lovingly reaches her arms around him. Seth rests his head on Laurie's head. The couple hug, exchanging energy and prayers in their thoughts.

"Seth…the girls and I have peace knowing you protect us. And part of that is making decisions that keep yourself out of harm's way."

Seth confides, "When I think of what happened to our daughter, I feel rage. Sometimes it overwhelms me." Seth kisses the top of Laurie's head. "I am blessed with your wisdom. Thank you."

Nicole comes down from her bedroom to have breakfast with her parents and her older sisters, who will be home for the week. Nicole and her parents bring Lisa and Kimberly up to speed on the events that have taken place. Both sisters are very protective and extremely furious.

"So, what about Nick? Are you going to leave him hanging or talk to him?" Lisa questions.

Nicole sighs. "I can't face him…and he made it CRYSTAL clear to Cami the wedding is off and NOT to contact him."

Lisa and Kimberly both curls their lips.

"I can't even imagine how devastating this is for you, sis. I am so sorry." Kimberly reaches and places her hand upon Nicole's hand.

"We have more news," Seth reveals to his daughters. "As of 9 a.m. this morning, our home phone and cell phone numbers will be disconnected. Well, to be more accurate, all the numbers will be changed. We are taking precautionary measures regarding the young man who attacked your sister. We are also moving. Your mother and I have been wanting a home in The Meadows, and it just so happens, there is one that is recently finished that your mother and I like. We put an offer in, it was accepted, and we move in at the end of the week."

"Wow! That is fast!" Lisa comments.

Laurie nods. "We are extremely fortunate that everything fell into place."

"Doesn't the guy live like three hours away?" Kimberly questions.

"Yes! But this is my way of protecting my family," Seth asserts.

"I like your ideas, Dad." Lisa nods. "What are you plans, or do you have any yet?" Lisa turns and casts her eyes upon Nicole.

"I don't know. Honestly, the past few weeks I have been completely unproductive and laying around," Nicole admits.

"That is alright. That is how our body and mind heals. Do not be so hard on yourself." Lisa gives a loving gaze at her sister.

"Yes. I agree. Don't be so hard on yourself. This is a big deal in your life. And we are all here for you," Kimberly assures.

"Did you report it to the authorities?" Lisa questions her younger sister.

"No. Nor am I," Nicole adamantly states. Nicole's voice perks up when she continues, "Sometime, I would like us all to drive to the convent and visit the sisters. They took such good care of me and gave me strength. I haven't decided what I want to do for my career, but something will come to me," Nicole outlines. "What happened still haunts me, plus the image of seeing Nick and that person in the drive…." Nicole sighs. "I still have no recollection as to…." Nicole stops.

"It's alright, dear," Laurie softly voices.

You can hear the forks clinking against the plates while the family slowly eats breakfast. Though their hearts are heavy, they savor every delicious bite of waffles, butter, syrup, biscuits, and gravy. What happens to one affects them all.

Nick casts a line into the lake. He attempts to keep his mind off images he imagines of Nicole with that guy.

Alex knows something is off. "So, I guess your trip to see Nicole didn't go so well?"

Nick shakes his head.

"Wanna talk about it?" Alex gently treads.

"Nope." Nick reels in his line and casts it out again.

Alex nods. The best friends continue to fish.

After nearly thirty minutes, Nick blurts out, "She had sex with another guy! I met him! He all but told me the details!"

"Wait! No way! That has got to be false!" Alex assures.

"No! It's true! I saw Nicole walking down the street. The guy spoke disrespectful…vulgar," Nick details.

"Nah, that definitely does NOT sound like the Nicole we know," Alex assures. "She would never go for a guy like that, or anyone for that matter. I'm telling ya, she is solely into you. You need to call her. You guys owe each other that. Heck, her parents and even yours have money tied up in your wedding. That, of course, is not a reason to marry, but it is one of the many reasons to search for the truth," Alex rationalizes.

Nick ponders. "Maybe you're right." Nick pauses. "Ya know, I punched that guy right in the gut with my left hook."

Alex releases a short laugh. "Now, that-*IS* the Nick I know." Alex grins from ear to ear.

"Yeah. He had it coming. I felt good, but then I felt bad that I harmed someone," Nick shares.

"Understandable." Alex nods, as he casts his line out.

"I'm gonna call her right now from my cell phone." Nick decides. He reaches for his phone and dials her number. "What am I gonna say? Shouldn't she be the one contacting me?" Nick holds the phone to his ear to listen. "Huh, that's weird, it's making a ringing sound, like it's been disconnected."

"Nah, it would say, 'I'm sorry, the number you are trying to reach is no longer in service…'" Alex imitates an automated response.

Alex and Nick both laugh.

"That's pretty funny, Alex." Nick smiles. "Weird though, I have never heard a busy signal like that. I will try again later, and I will call their home phone as well. You're right, Nicole and I need to talk."

Alex smiles. "I am the best man after all."

"You are indeed, the BEST man!" Nick glances at his best friend and pats him on the back.

"Are you still considering entering the seminary? You don't want to marry…have a family?" Nick asks.

"I do, but that is not how I believe God is calling me. My parish would be my family. I would be leading them all. I will be serving God as the apostles did. I am waiting for my acceptance letter. I am really excited about it!" Alex smiles.

Alex and Nick enjoy the day hanging at the lake.

"I hope she hasn't ghosted me, though I made it clear not to contact me." Nick thinks aloud.

"You may feel ghosted, though you requested no contact. She may feel haunted by what has happened…which you will not know until you visit with her!" Alex maintains. "Trust what you know about Nicole, what you grew to love…let your knowledge guide you, not your emotions. Only trust a fraction of what you see, and even less of what you hear."

Nick grins. "So, you do know who you are talking to?"

Alex gins and looks directly into the eyes of Nick. "Haha, I do."

CHAPTER 11

An Unexpected Turn

A few days pass. Alex is over at the home of Amy's parents, working on Amy's car. Amy carries Patrick outside.

"I sure appreciate you doing this," Amy conveys.

Alex raises his head from under the hood. "Aw, it's nothing. I'm glad I can help."

Amy smiles. "Yeah, me too."

"I have been meaning to tell you, thank you, for naming your little one after me. Well, his middle name." Alex peers at Amy.

"Patrick, my husband, would agree with my name selection," Amy states.

"Your husband sounds like he was a great guy." Alex nods and gets back to work. "I am almost done here."

"He was a great guy. I still believe you saved our lives. Clearly, me going into labor caused the crash, but you colliding with me was a blessing! The impact sent my car spinning safely into the median. So, thank you. You saved our lives!" Amy holds her baby, Patrick, close to her, and moves in a dancing movement.

"It is God that saved us," Alex firmly assures.

"Maybe angels. I don't know." Amy shrugs. "I don't know what I believe in anymore."

"For me, it is simple. God created us all in his likeness. His unique design…we are all different, yet the same. We can even donate organs. Our body tries to heal itself and does more than we realize. It's a masterpiece…designed by our Creator," Alex speaks matter-of-factly.

"I used to believe that way. I don't know anymore." Amy shrugs again.

"Tell ya what. Come to church with me sometime. You will see," Alex invites.

"I will think about it." Amy slightly smiles. "Well, I am going to take Patrick inside for a nap."

Alex walks over next to Amy and leans to speak directly to Patrick Alexander. "You have a good nap, little guy." Alex then stands straight up. "I will finish up, start it and let it run, and I will see you another day."

"Thank you, Alex. I sure appreciate you. And, Nick and Nicole. I am so glad I met you all," Amy relays.

"See, God led our paths together." Alex smiles.

"You and your God…." Amy slightly shakes her head.

"He led us so our paths would meet. He protects us. He has a plan for each of us," Alex evangelizes.

Amy ascends the concrete steps of her home, she glances back at Alex. "I'll keep that in mind."

Alex nods. "And I will take you and your son to church one of these weekends!"

Alex smiles and closes the hood of Amy's car. He goes over to the driver's door to get in. At that moment, Nick pulls into the driveway. Nick gets out of his car at the same time Alex steps back out of Amy's car.

"Hey, buddy, did you get it fixed?" Nick hollers as he walks toward Alex.

"You know it!" A large grin plasters across Alex's face. Alex reaches for an envelope from his inner pocket. "Look what I got in the mail this morning!"

"Is that what you have been hoping for?" Nick happily smiles.

"It Is! I was accepted into the seminary!" Alex exclaims with joy.

"Wow! Congratulations!" Nick and Alex embrace and bounce in a circle. "I won't feel so scared confessing my sins to you, Father Alex." Nick folds his hands in prayer and bows.

Smiles decorate the handsome faces of Nick and Alex. They both laugh.

"I am so proud of you, Alex!" Nick pats Alex on the back.

"Thanks, man! Any word from our girl?" Alex questions.

"Not a word. Their phone number *has* been disconnected. I have decided I am going to drive to Careyville to see what has happened," Nick informs.

"Yeah. It just does not make any sense. She is so totally in love with you," Alex expresses.

Nick sighs. "As I am with her. I don't know what happened. I don't know what I did that would make her want to be with someone else. And, I DID tell Cami to tell Nicole the wedding is off and not to contact me."

"Nick…I don't believe you did anything to cause this. I think something has happened," Alex maintains. "Like I told you when we were fishing, something does not add up. You need to find out."

"Why won't she tell me?" Nick ponders.

Alex shakes his head. "I don't know, buddy. But I do not believe any of this has anything to do you with you. I mean, I know it affects you, but I don't believe you are the root source." Alex takes a step. "Nick?"

"Yeah?" Nick questions.

"You know, I love you. I don't feel very…." Alex collapses during his sentence.

Nick instantly drops to his knees and positions his right arm under Alex's head and cradles him next to his body. "Alex! Alex!" Nick then cries out, "HELP! HELP!" Nick caresses the face of his best friend with his left hand.

Amy hears screaming through the open windows and comes out the front door. She views Alex lying in the arms of Nick, on the ground. "I'll call for help!" Amy runs through the house to the phone and dials, 9-1-1. Amy remains on the line answering the questions as best she can until they arrive.

EMS arrives and rushes to Nick holding Alex in his arms. "I think he is gone." Nick stares up at the paramedics and uncontrollably sobs.

Amy steps out onto the front porch and remains there.

The paramedics help secure Alex. Nick moves out of their way.

"What happened?" Kyle, one of the paramedics asks.

"I don't know. We were talking about cars and girls, then he said my name, told me he loved me, and that he doesn't feel very…but before he finished his sentence, he collapsed," Nick tries to accurately detail the events, but he chokes on his words. Tears stream down Nick's face.

CHAPTER 12

The Funeral

Laurie, Nicole's mother, receives a letter that is forwarded to their new address. It is from Emily, Nick's mother, informing her of the death of Alex. Laurie has no time to write that ensures a response letter will arrive before the funeral.

Alex's parent, Jack and Vickie, along with Alex's younger brother, Aaron, are escorted to the front pew. Relatives follow. Nick and his family follow and sit in the third pew from the front. The Monroe's and their relatives, fill the first two pews.

Seth, Laurie, and Nicole discreetly attend the funeral. Laurie and Nicole wear black veils that cover their faces. They enter the doors of the parish in time to sign the guest book and take a seat in the back pew.

Nicole tries not to look around, but does notice Amy holding her baby across the aisle and over some distance to the right.

The homily the priest communicates is precisely perfect detailing the life of Alex. Nicole is relieved to see that this parish offers communion for those seated in the back of the parish, to shorten the lines. Extraordinary ministers for each side come to the back, while the priest and one extraordinary minister remain at the front.

After the final blessing, when there is an opportune time, Nicole and her parents quietly slip out the back. Amy happens to glance over and recognizes Nicole's side profile even under the black veil.

"How about we go for lunch?" Seth suggests.

Laurie glances over at her husband driving and realizes even though she is not hungry, he may be, but moreover, he needs to get out of their truck and stretch. "I like that idea. Nicole, are you familiar with any good places to eat over here?"

From the backseat, Nicole leans frontwards. "Yeah, if you guys want steak, there is a place right up the road, turn left, go two blocks. And if you want Mexican food, well, actually, it is on the same road about another block."

Seth nods. "Thank you." Seth drives. He chooses a restaurant and backs into a parking stall. He and his family get out of the truck and walk in.

At the cemetery, after the burial words, Nick notices Amy walking toward her car, carrying Patrick. He increases his pace to catch up. "Hey, wait up."

"Are you going back to the parish for lunch?" Nick asks.

"No. We need to get home. Plus, I am all funeral'd out," Amy matter-of-fact states.

Nick slightly laughs. "Is that a word?"

"It is today. Look, I need to go. I am sorry about Alex." Amy places Patrick in the car seat and straps him in, then closes the door. "By the way, I thought you would want to know, Nicole and her parents were at the funeral."

"They were?" Nick is surprised.

"Yeah. Nicole and her mother were wearing black veils, but they were there for the entire funeral Mass." Amy moves with purpose to her driver's side.

Nick reaches to open the door for her.

Amy gets in. "I gotta go."

Nick steps back. "Thank you for coming."

Amy reaches to close her door, and rolls down her window about halfway. "It's the least I could do. He died as a result of the crash…that I caused." Amy starts her car, pulls the gear shifter into drive, and drives away.

Nick shakes his head. He then raises his arms, places his hands on top of his head, and takes a few steps around, and thinks, *maybe Alex is right, and I have the wrong information about Nicole. God, why did you take Alex? And Nicole, why did you break us?* Nick returns to his family. He then steps next to his best friend's parents and brother. They exchange hugs. The families return to the parish for lunch. The rest of the mourners at the burial site also return to the parish for the meal.

CHAPTER 13

Seeking Answers

Around ten days pass. Nick decides to drive to Careyville. He arrives in town and goes to their address. He pulls across the street. He notices some distinct changes and thinks to himself, *okay, those do not look like their vehicles, nor the same porch furniture. The yard does not appear as manicured.* Nick decides to get out of his car and go knock on the door.

A young woman, maybe in her thirties, answers the door. Toddlers are running around. "Hello, may I help you?"

"Ah, maybe I have the wrong address. I thought the Thompson family lives here," Nick politely communicates.

"Oh, yes, they were the previous owners. We purchased the home, I do not know where they moved. I'm sorry," the young mother states.

Nick nods. "Alright. Thank you." Nick descends the front porch steps and returns to his car. *Think man. That's it!* Nick drives to their favorite bakery in Careyville. *They know me and have seen me with Nicole. I'll just go buy something and ask.*

Nick arrives at the most delicious bakery in Careyville. He enters. Maria walks out from behind the counter. "Nicolas! So glad to see you! What can I serve you today?"

Nick orders his usual, Nicole's favorite, and something for her parents.

"Tell them I say 'Hello,' will you?" Maria bags up the pastries and sets them on the counter for Nick to take.

"Yes, what is the name of that street again?" Nick pretends he does not remember.

"Oh yes…it is in the new addition, you know, just north of town, called, The Meadows," Maria recalls.

"That's it! I am sure I will recognize the street once I get there." Nick nods.

"Oh, yes. I am sure of it." Maria cordially smiles, collects his money and voices, "You have a fine day with your people, Nicolas."

"Thank you, Maria." Nick turns to leave.

"Wait!" Maria requests. She again comes out from behind the counter. She gives Nick a big hug. "Good to see you, young man."

Nick smiles. "Thank you, Maria."

Nick opens the door and steps one foot out when he hears Maria holler, "And peace be to you, Nicholas." Nick nods and waves. He thinks to himself, *alright, I know, Alex, all kinds of things I need to confess. But you did tell me I needed to seek the truth, even though I sunk to deception to put me on the right track. This is just messed up. I don't even know WHAT to pray.* Nick drives to one of the main residential streets and heads north. *There are so many roads that head north. Maybe I can stop at a service station and ask.* Nick pulls into a service station he sees. Nick gets out and asks the attendant directions.

"Much obliged. Thank you." Nick waves at the attendant.

Nick returns to his car and proceeds to the directions given him. He turns into The Meadows. *Wow! Nice! Gravel roads. Look at these yards! It looks like each home sits on five to ten acres. Seth and Laurie will love this! I see why they moved. They have always thought about it.*

Nick follows the main road traveling at a very slow, neighborhood speed. He searches for a familiar vehicle. After a few minutes of driving the curvy roads in the area, and viewing a beautiful lake, he spies Seth's truck. He pulls over and watches, formulating in his head what he is going to say.

A truck pulls up in front of their home. A young man gets out. Nick watches. The gentleman pulls a bouquet of flowers from the seat and a gift box. *Who is this guy?* Just then, he spots Nicole walking from the house toward the well-dressed guy, who is wearing a sport jacket and jeans. *Hmm, she is walking toward him. Who IS he?* Nick continues to observe. *What?* Nick witnesses Nicole and the young man exchange a hug. The man hands her the bouquet of flowers and he carries the wrapped box. They stroll up the stone sidewalk to the front porch and enter. Nick places the fingers of his right hand on his forehead and rubs it. *I can't believe it. So...she HAS moved on.* Nick sighs, pulls away, and drives home.

"Derek! So good to see you!" Laurie hugs her nephew.

Nicole hands her mother the bouquet of flowers. "Aw, you are so sweet Derek. Thank you." Laurie smiles at her nephew.

"Here, this box is a housewarming present from mom and dad. They are sorry they could not come with me today. Mom wants me to tell you she and dad will come down next week." Derek takes off his jacket.

"Yes, my sister has such a busy schedule!" Laurie conveys.

"How's my favorite cousin?" Derek asks Nicole.

"Shh, don't let my sisters hear you!" Nicole giggles.

"Oh! Did they make it in?" Derek questions.

"Yes. Last night," Laurie informs.

"Very good. Well, Mom and Dad are gonna be disappointed if they miss seeing them!" Derek communicates.

Seth walks in from the other room. "All things will work out. How are you, Derek?" Seth greets his nephew with a hug.

"I am good, Uncle Seth." Derek peers into the eyes of his uncle.

"Get your bag, and I will show you to your room," Seth directs.

"On it." Derek grins and walks back outside to get his bag.

"I love our family gatherings." Laurie hugs Seth.

"I do, too." Seth embraces his wife.

Nicole, and her sisters step outside into the backyard of their parent's new home, their family home. The sisters spread out and notice all the details their parents have already put into the landscape.

"Aww, look over here!" Lisa points.

Kimberly and Nicole stroll over to Lisa. The sisters beam with joy when they see the stepping stones their parents made for them when they were little. One reads; Lisa Marie Thompson. Kimberly Anne Thompson is etched into the second stone. Carved into a third stone, is the name, Nicole Elizabeth Thompson.

"That is so great they dug these up from our other home and brought them here." Lisa glances at her sisters.

"I love our family." Kimberly wraps her arms around both sisters and pulls them close to her. Kimberly then voices to Nicole, "Don't worry, Nicole, everything is truly going to work out."

"It is," Lisa affirms.

Nicole nods and gazes with love to both of her sisters.

CHAPTER 14

Letting it out

Nick arrives home. He drags himself out of his car and into his home.

Paul and Emily are at the dining room table.

"Son, come and join us." Paul greets Nick.

Nick saunters into the dining area, scratches his head, and sits down.

"Can I get you something? Water? Milk?" Emily asks.

"No." Nick sighs.

"Well? How did it go? Did you get to see her?" Paul inquires.

"Oh yeah. I saw her, alright…hug some guy that brought her flowers and a present," Nick describes.

"Aw, honey, that could have been anybody," Emily comforts.

"No, I don't think so. He was dressed nice. Nicole and him hugged. She took the bouquet from him and they strolled up the sidewalk, up the stairs and into her new home." Nick flings his arms about. "I went to the home I knew of…the one we have visited many times…but no…no longer their home. They sold it. So, not only did they turn off their phones so I could not contact

Nicole, they moved. Which prompted me to stop in the bakery and purchase some pastries. I KNEW Maria would point me in the right direction. Of course, she assumed a lot, and I took advantage of that, which is deceitful. SIN…I better make an appointment for confession; I am going to be there for some time." Nick sighs.

His parents exchange a look with each other. Emily gets up and goes to the kitchen to pour Nick a glass of milk. She returns and sets it in front of him, then sits back down.

Paul and Emily are in disbelief.

"Honestly, son, I am sure there is a reasonable explanation for everything. It may not have anything at all to do with you," Paul suggests.

Nick sets his elbows on the table and places his forehead in his hands and massages his forehead. "I don't know. This entire thing feels like it is about me. Like it IS personal." Nick continues to firmly massage his forehead. "Alex told me the same thing, though. I don't know. I thought I knew how my life was going to unfold. Marry Nicole, Alex as our best man. Alex becoming a priest, me becoming a father…none of that is happening." Nick repositions himself. He folds his arms on the table in front of him and drops his head into his arms. He loudly cries out.

Emily and Paul exchange eye contact. Emily wants to reach over and rub her son's back. Paul slightly shakes his head signaling not to. Emily and Paul feel deep compassion for their son. They recognize he needs to experience a moment of mourning by himself before they reach to embrace and comfort him.

Nick bawls out raw emotion from so much heart break that he has experienced over the course of a short time. Paul and Emily both get up and pull out a chair on each side of Nick. Each parent sits down next to Nick. They both lean in to embrace their son and offer prayers.

CHAPTER 15

Moving On

Nick drives over to Amy's. He parks his new truck and ambles up to the door.

"Well, hi, Nick. Come on in." Amy opens the door. How are you doing?"

"As good as could be expected, I guess," Nick delivers.

"Yeah, death is tough," Amy voices.

"It is. But I was referring to Nicole," Nick replies. "I have lost them both!"

"Oh. Right. Well, like I told you the last time you visited, when you told me what you saw, hey, man…you have eyes. Trust what you see." Amy steers Nick in the wrong direction.

"Really?" Nick raises an eyebrow.

"Well, sure. God gave us two eyes," Amy maintains. "Hey, I made dinner if you want to stay and eat."

Nick nods. "I guess so." Nick steps over to Patrick who is lying on a large blanket in the center of the floor.

"He can roll over now." Amy hollers from the kitchen.

"Hey Patrick Alexander…you're moving pretty good there." Nick smiles and touches Patrick.

Patrick coos and makes baby sounds. Nick smiles. "Do you need any help?"

"Not tonight," Amy relays.

Amy sets the table for two, and carries the main course and sides to the table. She also brings in a pitcher of tea. "I hope you like tea."

"I do." Nick nods.

"Cool. Well, sit down." Amy extends her arm and points.

Nick sits down. "This is nice. Thank you."

"Well, feeding you is the least I can do to repay you for all your help with my car or the yard or the house." Amy smiles and reaches her hand out and places her hand on top of Nick's hand.

Nick and Amy exchange eye contact. Nick realizes it is not the same as his eye contact with Nicole. Nicole and he could exchange unspoken sentences through their eye contact.

"Hey, I have an idea. Marry me. We are both alone. We have both suffered extreme losses. Patrick needs a dad. I am helping you around the house anyway. I won't be home much because I am working full time AND going to college. Things may be tough for a while, but why not?" Nick proposes.

"Wow. Well, like a partnership? Like trauma bonds, except good. We are both hurt. Both lost our true loves…both are here anyway. Sure. Why not?" Amy nods.

"I do believe there is more than one person for everybody. Some people may have two or three people they truly love. But for me…like you…for now…you had Patrick…I had Nicole," Nick reasons.

"Yes. But I like your idea. We will complete the needs of each other." Amy speculates. "Alright. When do you want to get married?"

"I don't know…why wait?" Nick questions. "Well, it is important to me to get married in the Catholic Church."

"That works, since I am a widow and you have never been married. I think we are required to fill out some paperwork and attend a weekend," Amy assumes.

"Alright. I will let my parents and our parish priest know. I will find out how soon." Nick stands. "Thank you, for dinner. I am gonna go. I have a lot to do."

Amy stands. "Alright."

"Wait, I'll help you clear dishes." Nick gathers dishes from the table and carries them into the kitchen. He helps clean up. He has observed his dad enough times help his mother, like teamwork. So that is what he mimics.

"Well, that made short work of things. Thank you." Amy smiles.

"I remember seeing my dad most always help my mom. They both helped each other, that way it freed them both up to do whatever they wanted…quicker. For instance, like dad watching half a movie before mom could join him. I think they decided to help each other early on. I always remember my parents helping each other," Nick recalls.

"That's beautiful." Amy escorts Nick to the door.

"Okay, I'll see you later!" Nick feels a little awkward and then leans in to kiss Amy's cheek. "Okay, bye." He turns. "Be safe." Nick descends the steps and gets into his truck. *Oh, that's great! What did I just do? It's alright. It makes sense. Alex is gone, Nicole is gone, well, with someone else, and Patrick is gone. I am not physically attracted to Amy though. How is THAT going to work? Do we have to have a physical relationship?* Thoughts race through Nick's head while he drives home.

Laurie retrieves mail out of the mail box, like she does most days when she is done with her walk. She flips through the mail and notices familiar handwriting addressed to her. Laurie stops to tear open the envelope. She reads the hand-written letter,

Dear Laurie, I want to extend my thanks to you so much for attending Alex's funeral. He was like our son. His family is strong in their faith, but still, it is a difficult time.

On another matter, we love your family as our own. We are very saddened for the direction Nick and Nicole took. We hope Nicole is very happy with the new man in her life. Nick drove to your new home about ten days after the funeral and told us he saw a handsome man with a present and a bouquet of flowers…and that he and Nicole exchanged a hug and Nicole carried the bouquet of flowers into the house.

Anyway, we do love Nicole, and hope all the very best for you all! For whatever happened between Nick and Nicole, as I said, it fills our hearts with sorrow.

With that being said, Nick and Amy got married. Yes, we were surprised as well! He said to Paul and I, 'the baby needs a dad. Alex, and Amy's husband, Patrick, are dead, and Nicole moved on…so why not?' were his exact words. Maybe you can let Nicole know.

We miss you and Seth!

Our love and Prayers,

Paul & Emily Parks.

Laurie's eyes widen. She cannot believe what she read. She hurries inside her home to the office. She reaches for her stationary and a pen to respond to Emily.

Oh, Dear Emily,

It is so good to hear from you! Seth and I miss the both of you as well, plus, Nick and Nicole as a couple! What happened between them, well, they should have sought each other out to communicate. The handsome man Nick believes to be Nicole's new boyfriend, is her cousin, my nephew, my sister's son. We were having a housewarming gathering. Nicole does not have another man in her life. In the beginning, she spent most days in her room, she even wanted to change her appearance, but we convinced her not to. It is only recently that she is surfacing from the depths of despair she was stuck in. We are extremely relieved that she rarely mentions she wishes God would kill her. We encouraged her to enroll in the local college and live at home for now. She thought both were good ideas. Nicole enrolled in the local college here and decided to remain living at home for the time being. Her older sisters are making more trips home to hang out with her. So, family time right now is healing time.

We wish Nick all the best. He will certainly make an excellent dad and husband!

Our love & prayers,

Laurie & Seth

Laurie folds the letter, places it in the envelope, seals it, places a stamp on it, addresses the envelope, then stands up. She folds the letter she received and places it in her pocket. She carries the letter she is going to mail, grabs her keys from the kitchen, goes to the garage, and drives out. (Because they always back into their garage.)

Laurie drives to the post office to drop the letter in outgoing mail for the day. She then decides to go to the grocery store since she is in town.

CHAPTER 16

Dinner Conversations

Emily receives the letter from Laurie. She reads the letter and shakes her head. She prepares dinner for her and Paul.

Emily greets Paul with a kiss when he walks in. "Good day?"

Paul nods and smiles. "Something smells delicious."

"Well, I decided to make homemade pizza tonight. It's Friday night, I figure pizza, followed by a movie and popcorn." Emily winks. She carries the pizza to the table and places it on a trivet.

Paul reaches for a beer in the refrigerator. "What do you want to drink?"

"How about a coke." Emily smiles. "Always good with pizza." Emily sits down. "No, make it a root beer, please."

"I can do that." Paul expresses a slight chuckle. He sets the drinks on the table. "How was your day?"

"Wonderful. I received a letter from Laurie," Emily tells.

"I miss that family." Paul takes a bite of his pizza and gives a thumbs up.

Emily smiles.

"You did tell her about Nick getting married?" Paul asks.

"I did." Emily nods. "In the last letter I wrote. You know, I think the decisions Nick has made has been a result of assumptions, not facts. Here, read the letter, see what you think." Emily pulls out the folded letter from her pocket and hands it to Paul.

Paul reads the letter, and takes a drink of his beer. He sighs. His facial expression appears to be somber. "From reading this, I think Nicole was assaulted."

"Yes, that is the impression I get as well." Emily stares at Paul.

Paul glances over the letter again and shakes his head. "There was no other man, that was her cousin!" He peers at Emily. "Our son has made life decisions from assumptions and not facts!"

"I know. Everything he thinks he knows, is inaccurate." Emily shrugs and curls her lips. "Do you think we should tell him?"

Paul and Emily both extend their arms toward one another and hold hands for a few moments. Paul takes another bite of the delicious pizza, and a drink of his beer.

"No. He is already married to Amy. I don't believe there is an attraction, but they fill a void the other needs. No, Nick will find out the truth if he is meant to, and we will not interfere." Paul slightly shakes his head. "If what he believes torments him, he should have sought the truth without being so hasty. In addition, he has led us and many others to believe the worst about Nicole."

"I know. I feel so heartbroken for Nicole. She never intentionally ghosted Nick; she was processing and healing from a trauma," Emily adds.

"If our son was not such a hothead, and sought the truth, we would have Nicole as our daughter-in-law." Paul takes another bite of pizza and dabs the corners of his mouth with a napkin."

"I agree. I pray he grows out of his quick reactions," Emily voices.

"I agree, I think he will manage his anger differently as he matures. Man, all these assumptions he formed, well, it has really caused the two of them to be thrown off course," Paul expresses.

Emily sighs. "I know. Alright, second topic, I would love for us to keep in contact with Nicole, but I think it is best if we only keep in contact with her parents, at least for now. What do you think?"

"I like the idea of having barbeques or going boating with Seth and Laurie, or even playing cards, or meeting for dinner somewhere. But Nick, nor Nicole can know. And I agree, as much as I would like for us to remain an active part of Nicole's life, we will pray for her and watch from a distance. God will reunite us all in his time," Paul discloses his sentiments. "We must show support to Nick, Amy, and Patrick."

Emily nods. "Yes. Okay, I agree. I cannot even imagine how devastated Nicole must feel, and to be so misunderstood by our son. He is not going to be happy with himself when he does find out."

"Well, maybe by the time he finds out, he will be older and wiser. You know, things will work out, or they won't." Paul takes a drink of his beer. "And this will be a good lesson to him that communication is key. He made hasty decisions based on assumptions." Paul pauses. "Which has affected everyone!" Paul takes the last bite of his third piece of pizza. "Anything else?"

"No, I just wish you and I could visit Nicole and give her our love," Emily voices.

"Yeah, I do too." Paul carries his plate to the sink, rinses it, and sets it in the dishwasher. He throws his beer bottle into the trash. "Movie thoughts?"

"Yeah, romance-comedy, NO Drama!" Emily laughs.

Paul smiles and winks.

"Hang on, let me make some popcorn." Emily grabs a pan. She sets it on the stove, adds some oil and popcorn, places the lid on it, and turns on the heat.

Paul gets butter out and melts some in the microwave while the popcorn cooks on the stove.

"I like our movie nights." Emily smiles at Paul.

"I do, too! I'll grab us each a root beer and some napkins." Paul gets to it. He pulls the melted butter from the microwave and pours the butter over the popcorn that is now in a large bowl.

Their hands are full carrying drinks, napkins, and popcorn. They retreat to the family room to watch a movie that will bring them laughter.

CHAPTER 17

Paths Cross

Around fourteen years pass. A new park has been designed and built, next to Lake Belinay (which means: reflection of the moon on the water) for people to enjoy in Kenny County. Today, the landscape architectural firm that designed the park, along with the marketing company that received donations and matched every donation, are hosting a ribbon-cutting ceremony.

Nick, his parents, his sister, along with her husband and children attend. Cami is joined by her husband Carl. People from all over the large county are in attendance.

Nick spies Cami and strolls over to her through the crowd. He comes up from behind and stands beside her. "Some crowd, huh?" Nick voices.

Startled, Cami turns her head to look next to her. "Nick! Wow! It has been years!" Then she reaches to her husband on the other side and taps his arm. "Carl, I would like you to meet Nick. I met Nick the end of my senior year."

"Of college?" Carl questions.

"No." Cami giggles. "Of high school."

"Ooooh!" Carl smiles, raises his head up and lowers it down, and chuckles.

Carl and Nick cordially smile and exchange a firm handshake.

"Nice to meet you, Nick. Hey, I'm going to find my parents and take the boys off their hands." Carl winks at Cami. "I'll be back shortly."

"Sure thing, babe." Cami and Carl exchange a quick kiss.

"He seems like a good man," Nick comments.

"He is. I am very fortunate to have met him. Our sons are nine and twelve," Cami shares.

"That must keep you two busy," Nick makes conversation.

"It does. What about you?" Cami asks.

"Well, I went to the local college, got my degree, became a paramedic, and eventually fire chief for the area I live," Nick details.

"Wow! A real-life hero! That is great, Nick! Where is Amy…and didn't she have a son?" Cami inquires.

"Yes. Well, Amy does not like to get out. Plus, she is not feeling well. And Patrick is fifteen," Nick answers.

"That's great! Did you have any other children?" Cami questions.

"No." Nick glances around at the crowd.

"Yeah, she is here with her husband and family," Cami reveals.

"Is she happy? Does she laugh?" Nick inquires.

Cami stares at Nick. "Yes, I believe she is happy. Does she laugh? I don't know. Yeah, sometimes…sure. She tends to be on the serious side of things. Surely, you remember. I think that is one of the many reasons she loved you so much. You had a way about you that brought laughter to her serious tendencies." Cami pauses and observes Nick's facial expressions. "Her husband is the senior landscape architect for the firm that was hired for this park project." Cami peers at Nick.

Nick nods. "Okay, I can see that."

"Wait a minute…what is that supposed to mean?" Cami gets defensive.

Nick shrugs. "I just mean, that makes sense. She came from money. I went to look for her only to find out they had moved into the estates north of town. You know, The Meadows. She searched for a guy with money."

"Are you for real? That is NOT who Nicole is…AT ALL! You know NOTHING Nick Parks!" Cami scoffs. "When did you start to believe things you KNOW are not true?"

"I call it like I see it," Nick retorts. "Plus, I drove over to visit with her. I saw her new boyfriend handing her a bouquet of flowers and a gift. It appeared pretty clear to me, she had moved on, so I married Amy."

"Wait." Cami tilts her head and raises one hand in the air and slightly twists her wrist. "When exactly do you think you saw this so-called boyfriend?"

"Oh, I don't know. Maybe one or two weeks after Alex's funeral," Nick recalls.

Cami thinks and then the memory is clear as day. "You dope! That was her cousin! He brought flowers for Nicole's mother, who is his aunt, and a house warming gift! I was there that weekend, along with her sisters, relatives…it was a house warming weekend!" Cami verifies. "You are so argumentative! You assume things instead of verifying! You call it like you SEE it? Didn't anyone ever teach you to believe only a fraction of what you see and less of what you hear!" Cami chastises!

Nick inhales and exhales. He sighs. "As a matter-of-fact, yes. Alex did."

Cami sighs as well. "Alex was the best!"

Nick nods. "He was."

"Look, all of us have taken some pretty hard hits. But you don't have a clue about Nicole! So, get out of your imagination that clearly leads you south and search for truth!" Cami's eyebrows furrow and her forehead creases. "Nice to see you, Nick." Cami, agitated, storms away to join her family.

Nick shakes his head and thinks to himself, *to this day I get so wound up. All I ever wanted was to give Nicole the very best. To provide a home for her, a place she would thrive. We truly balanced each other. I need to pull myself together. I have enjoyed a blessed life, and have accomplishments to be proud of. Everyone experiences heart ache and loss. You are not special Nick Parks.* Nick chortles a little listening to his thoughts. Nick tries to digest what Cami just informed him of; that Nicole did not have a boyfriend. He places one hand on his head and rubs from front to back once and thinks to himself, *all these years...what I believed...is not true. Wow! I made life choices based on assumptions. Oh my.* Nick sighs, realizing the magnitude of his choices from believing his assumptions without verification.

CHAPTER 18

I Am Here

About twelve years pass by. An emergency call for help comes in through dispatch. The local fire chief hears it and is close to the address given. He jumps into his red pick-up truck. His crew is already on the way while returning from another call. The fire crew that arrives at the country home consists of one paramedic and one EMT. They enter the glass screen door and search the home. They see a lady lying in her bed and rush in.

"How can we help? What is the problem?" Roger, the paramedic questions.

"I don't know. I am so dizzy, I can't stand," Nicole voices. She leans over.

Stan, the EMT, takes her vitals.

The fire chief arrives and enters the house.

"I'm gonna throw up," Nicole informs.

Stan, grabs a trash can and hands it to Nicole. She leans over the end of her bed and begins vomiting and crying. She feels very embarrassed.

"In here, Chief," Roger hollers.

Chief walks into the bedroom and cannot believe his eyes. He rushes and steps in front of the crew to be at her side. Nicole has her head leaning over the bed, vomiting, and crying, all the while, trying to hold her hair back.

Nick, the Fire Chief, reaches with one hand and gently takes a hold of her hair to hold it back. He tenderly places his other hand on her back and quietly voices, "I am here. You're gonna be alright. I won't let anything happen to you."

Nicole recognizes that voice. That voice that soothes her soul and calms her spirit. She wonders, *could it be? Why would he be here?* She throws up again.

"Bring me a couple of wet washrags," Nick directs to one of the crew.

Stan steps into the master bathroom, grabs two clean washrags, dampens them, wrings both out, and carries the washrags to the Chief.

Nick quietly voices, "I have a washrag when you are ready." He continues to firmly, but gently keep his hand on her back.

"Okay, I'm ready." Nicole raises her head.

He sweetly smiles at her and hands her the washrags. "One is for your mouth; one is for your head."

She wipes her mouth, and places the other washrag on her forehead and lies back.

"Have you been sick?" Nick asks.

"Not that I know of. I just became so dizzy. I have never experienced that," Nicole details.

"We are going to take you to the hospital. They will draw some blood work to figure out what is going on. You're in no shape to drive yourself," Nick quietly and calmly outlines.

Nicole nods and closes her eyes and drifts off to sleep. The crew carefully lifts her and securely places her on the stretcher and wheels her out. Nick walks beside her the entire way from her home to the ambulance. "You're gonna be just fine."

Nicole can hear Nick's soothing voice, but doesn't have the strength to open her eyes.

Though Nick wants to ride in the ambulance with her, he follows in his truck to the hospital.

The lab tech draws some blood for lab work the emergency room doctor orders. Within a short time, they determine Nicole has a urinary tract infection.

"Nicole, you have a urinary tract infection. Do you get those often?" Doctor Rhynes asks.

Nicole shakes her head. "I have never had one in my entire life."

"Have you experienced a fever, abdominal pain, frequent urination….?" Doctor Rhynes questions.

Nicole shakes her head to everything he voices. "No. Nothing."

"Alright. Well, I am going to give you an antibiotic to take now. That will be enough for today. I will write you a prescription. I want you to get it filled and begin tomorrow. Follow-up with your regular doctor next week," Doctor Rhynes instructs. "Do you have any questions?"

"No. Thank you," Nicole conveys.

"Do you have someone to drive you home?" Doctor Rhynes inquires.

"Yes. I will." Nick stands tall.

"Alright. You take care, Miss." Doctor Rhynes nods and turns to leave.

Nick looks at Nicole. He just smiles at her. "You are as beautiful now, if not more so, than when we were kids."

Nicole, still wanting to nod off, whispers, "And your voice still calms me."

Nicole falls asleep while they wait for the dismissal paperwork. Once the nurse brings it in, Nick gently places his hand on Nicole's arm to wake her. "Hey, I'm going to take you home now."

Nicole opens her eyes and nods.

The nurse assists Nicole into the wheelchair. The nurse wheels Nicole to the exit, through the doors, and to where Nick points. "That is my truck."

Nicole stands. The nurse wheels the chair back to the emergency room. Nick assists Nicole into his truck.

Nicole is groggy and sleepy from a medication they gave her to calm her nerves. She leans her head onto Nick. He nods. Many thoughts dance through his head during the return drive to her home. Nick escorts Nicole into her home and to her bedroom. Nick helps Nicole get into her tall bed.

"I'm sorry I don't feel like talking…because I sure would like to." Nicole lies back and rolls over. She closes her eyes and drifts.

Nick whispers, "You know we don't need words. Your eyes tell me everything." An expression of genuine concern paints Nick's face. Nick reaches for a blanket and covers Nicole. He removes her shoes and sets them on the floor, out of the way, so she does not trip when she gets up. Nick finds the kitchen, searches for a glass, fills it with water, and returns to the master bedroom. He sets the glass of water on the night stand. Nick places one hand on the blanket where her calf is located. "You rest. You're gonna be alright. Goodnight."

Nick quietly steps across the carpet of the bedroom to the door. He hears a quiet voice whisper, "I love you. Goodnight." He stops, turns his head, and glances back. A soft smile forms on his face. Nick's eyes gaze with love and care upon the sleeping beauty, Nicole.

CHAPTER 19

Knock at the Door

A week or so passes by. Memories haunt Nick. Sadness and anger creep into his spirit. He drives over to Nicole's home. He steps out of his truck and treks up to the door and rings the bell.

Nicole opens the door. She lights up when she sees him. "Well, hello! What a surprise! It was such a nice surprise to see you the other night! I am so sorry I was so sick! How embarrassing. But thank you, so much, for taking such good care of me!" Nicole conveys with energy.

"It was my pleasure. I am glad I could help. You were pretty groggy when I brought you home. I hope you slept well," Nick comments.

"I did. Thank you!" Nicole expresses. "Again, thank you for taking such good care of me."

"You're welcome. You know I always…." Nick chokes on his feelings. Nick becomes silent. He is battling a surge of emotions.

Trauma triggers rampantly rush Nicole from memories all those years ago. She steps back.

Nick and Nicole stare into the eyes of each other. It is as if they can still communicate without words. They can feel each other's heart-including each other's pain.

"Well, I better go." Nick nods.

"Alright. Thank you for checking in on me, AND for taking care of me!" Nicole sweetly voices.

"It's my pleasure." Nick gazes into Nicole's eyes. He then turns to leave.

Nicole closes the door and locks it. She looks around her home, and then heads to her bedroom. She thinks to herself, *what a way to reconnect! I miss him! We have missed out on so many years! He is such a good man!* Nicole climbs into her bed, though it is mid-day, and covers herself with blankets. She wants to take a nap to reset the trauma memories and heartache of longing for him. Her sweet dogs quickly surround her.

Nick treks down the steps of her front porch and across the brick sidewalk to the gravel driveway. Overwhelmed with emotions, he kicks some rocks, and smacks the palm of his hand onto the top of his truck when he notices a vehicle pulling in. The vehicle pulls around him and continues further into the drive onto a concrete slab in front of the garage. Two young females get out.

"Hello, can we help you?" Lily, the older one, asks.

Lily, and her sister, Olivia, approach the man by his truck, not knowing who he is.

"Who are you?" Nick asks. He conceals his feelings of hurt.

An inquisitive look casts upon the faces of both girls.

"I think we just asked you a question first," Olivia states.

Nick notices how the girls very much resemble Nicole.

"I am the fire chief of this area. The other day we had a call here, and I was just doing a follow-up." Nick attempts to come up with a plausible story.

"What? Is our mother alright?" Olivia quizzes.

"Yes. She is just fine. I was just checking in," Nick contends.

"Aw, that is so sweet. Just another reason my mother wanted to move here." Lily offers. "My name is Lily." Lily extends her hand to shake the hand of Nick.

"My name is Olivia." Olivia also offers her hand to firmly shake the hand of Nick.

"Well, it's very nice to meet you girls." Nick's hurt emotions subside.

"We wanted to come home and surprise mom this weekend," Olivia shares.

"Oh?" Nick questions.

"Yeah, we both go to the state university and School of Veterinarian. We are in our fourth year," Lily informs.

"Very good," Nick comments.

The sisters smile.

"In four more years, we will be veterinarians. We plan to open a practice together," Olivia voices.

"Wow! Sounds like you girls have aspirations." Nick is impressed. "Do either of you have a young man in your life?"

Lily laughs. "No. We are both focusing on our careers."

"Especially after learning what happened to our mother," Olivia communicates.

Lily shoots a look at Olivia.

"It's okay, it is a big deal and changed mother's life," Olivia presses.

Lily nods.

"Well, don't repeat this. Mother does not know that we know. Our grandmother told us years ago. We were visiting her and grandfather before we left for college," Olivia pauses.

"Apparently, our mom fell in love with someone at the end of her senior year of high school. They planned to marry, even had a date set, and wedding paid for. Both sets of parents embraced the notion and all of them meshed so incredibly well. Two days before mother left for college, the boy who was to be their best man, was in a tragic accident. He later died. Right after the accident, but before his death, mother had agreed to go to a party with her friend, Cami. It was then it happened." Lily stops.

"A guy drugged a glass of lemonade he handed to our mom, then he carried her off to his room," Olivia adds.

Nick is listening intensely. Memories flash through his head like a reel, *running into a guy at Nicole and Cami's, seeing Nicole down the street in tears and disarray. He sees himself shaking his head, getting into his car, and speeding away.* With every word he hears in each sentence of the story, his heart sinks. His wounds not only reopen but he realizes what he thought he knew and believed, was, indeed, all wrong.

"According to my grandmother, grandfather changed their home phone number, cell phone numbers, and they even moved. Grandmother says mom was a mess. Grandmother says mom was saving herself for her wedding day with the guy she met and loved…." Lily recounts.

"And now, after that, it was ruined. Grandmother said mom felt so unworthy of her fiancé, that she never told him. According to our grandmother, mother was ashamed. No doubt that mom felt robbed and a great loss of something she was saving to experience with her fiancé on their wedding night," Olivia discloses.

"Anyway, our grandmother gave us very strict guidelines about being safe. So, we follow them the best we can." Lily shrugs.

"I think that summer and fall shaped my mother into the woman she is today…I mean, grandmother told us our mother was very determined and loving since she was a young age, but we believe all that horrific trauma in a short time, imprinted her into becoming the inspiration she is today," Olivia explains.

"No doubt," Nick quietly voices.

"Anyway, we are hoping mom will meet a man like her first love. He sounds like a gem…and he totally loved her. So, that is what we hope for her…is that she meets someone like him. Someone that makes her feel so secure and loved." Lily smiles.

Nick nods. "What about your dad?"

"Oh, he passed away before we were out of high school from a heart attack," Olivia informs.

"Aw, I am sorry to hear that. And your mother has not met anyone?" Nick wonders.

"Ha, no. our mother will not date anyone! She tells all the suitors 'no'." Olivia laughs.

"Wow," Nick voices, and slightly shakes his head. "That is quite a powerful story. She should write a book about it."

"I think she has tried. Our grandparents encouraged her to, as part of the healing process, but the wounds were still fresh, and she never touched that project again to our knowledge," Lily expresses.

"Wow. Remarkable." Nick feels astonishment. He also feels ashamed for not seeking out the truth all those years ago.

"Well, I better go. I have other calls to make," Nick voices.

"Oh, we are sorry to share all this with you. Wow. Please, as we mentioned, our mom does not know we know. If you speak with her again, do not let her know," Lily requests.

Nick nods his head. "I won't." Nick pauses. "It is sure nice to meet both of you. Good luck on your studies and goals."

Olivia and Lily both smile at Nick.

"Thank you. It is nice to meet you." Olivia nods.

"Yes. And I am sorry we just spilt the beans about family secrets." Lily rolls her lips.

"Yeah, to someone we don't even know!" Olivia shakes her head.

"I have found that sometimes, that is the best source…and perhaps needed. I hope you two feel better." Nick raises his hand to the brim of his hat and nods. "You girls be safe." Nick steps into his truck and backs into the turnaround in the drive. He proceeds to drive out the long, curvy country driveway.

"He seems nice." Lily reaches for a suitcase out of the rear of the car.

"Yeah, I like him, too. But I noticed a wedding band." Olivia curls her lips.

"He looks so familiar. Like I have seen him." Lily sifts through her memory data.

"Let's go surprise mom." Olivia glows.

"Yes." Lily nods.

The girls use their key to unlock the door and enter their home. All is quiet. Even the dogs do not bark. The girls quietly tiptoe to their mother's bedroom and peek in. They see her sleeping.

"Aw, the dogs are curled up. She must have needed a nap." Olivia smiles.

"Come mere." Lily motions.

"What?" Olivia asks.

"I am going to glance through mother's drawings. I KNOW I have seen that fire chief's face before. I just cannot place it." Lily is on a mission.

"Maybe church?" Olivia suggests.

Lily and Olivia begin to flip through wrapped paintings and drawings of their mother's beautiful art work that rest in boxes. Mostly of landscapes. Some drawings are of pets, horses, and people.

Olivia gasps.

Lily glances over to her sister. "What did you find?"

Olivia peers at her sister, then into the box. She places a hand on each side of a picture that is wrapped with some type of a clear material that resembles cellophane. It sits between two pictures, in a box of many. Olivia carefully removes a drawing of a young man with dark brunette hair and brown eyes. "Is this him? Maybe, when he was younger?"

"Oh, my goodness." Lily carefully takes the picture into both of her hands. "It is! I can see the resemblance!"

"I think it is him, too!" Olivia declares and reaches for the picture. Olivia carefully turns the picture over to see if their mother titled it, like she does most of her artwork. “Look!” Olivia positions the drawing between her and Lily.

Together, the girls read aloud the hand-written cursive words, *Nick, you captured my heart with your wit, you kept my heart with your love. Forever, Nicole.*

The girls sit back and rest on their calves and gaze into each other’s eyes.

“Wow!” Lily shakes her head.

“Wow is right! Oh no! We just inadvertently told Nick what really happened,” Olivia expresses.

“You know what?” Lily pats Olivia on her thigh. “It’s alright. He even said sometimes things need to be shared, even with strangers. For whatever reason, I believe the Holy Spirit put it upon our hearts to share what happened...and to him, of all people! That is divine intervention! That is what I believe,” Lily imparts.

After Nicole’s daughters study the beautiful drawing of the handsome young man, Olivia gently places it back between the two drawings she pulled it from.

Olivia decides to finger through more drawings. She pulls out another one. “Wow! This guy is handsome!”

Lily studies the picture Olivia is holding. “Turn it over, who is it?”

Olivia reads aloud, *“Alex, you are truly our Best Man! With your natural gift of evangelization, and great love for Our Lord, you would have made a very inspirational priest. Our hearts are thankful we knew you. I will forever hold you as our best man, Father Alexander Jackson Monroe.”*

The sisters stare at each other.

“Let’s look at the next one,” Olivia suggests. She gingerly places the drawing of Alex behind the one of Nick. Olivia pulls out the next picture. The sisters giggle.

“That is a great picture of Mom and Cami!” Lily beams.

Olivia sets that picture back, and retrieves the next one. “Oh gosh! Look! It’s Aunt Lisa, Aunt Kimberly, and mom!”

"This is like going down memory lane of Mom's life!" Lily smiles.

"I know! This is great!" Olivia voices.

The girls reach for the next picture when they hear a noise.

Olivia and Lily quickly scoot the boxes back against the wall of their mother's art room and sneak out.

"Do you think Mom is awake?" Olivia asks.

"I don't know, it may be the dogs." Lily's eyes widen.

The sisters keep their voices down while they tread quietly to their bedrooms to drop off their bags.

"I bet you're right. Maybe ***he*** needed to hear what happened," Olivia proposes.

"Yes, for sure! Okay, let's get settled in our rooms and bake a dessert for Mom if she is still asleep," Lily suggests.

All sorts of emotions paired with feelings, flood Nick. He decides to drive around on dirt roads. Nick spies the turnoff to one of the lake entrances. He follows the lake road until there is a pull-off that leads near to the lake's edge. Nick gets out of his truck and hikes down to the shoreline. He reflects on the words Nicole's daughters spoke.

Nick thinks to himself, *I can't believe I didn't seek the truth all those years ago. Alex told me that I should. My parents encouraged me to. Man, was I stubborn when I was young! My assumptions robbed Nicole and I of a life together. I can't be with her now, I am married. I would not have an affair, that would offer her nothing and lead us both into sin. Maybe it was perfect timing that Nicole's daughters shared the truth with me, although, they didn't even know who I was. Perhaps the Holy Spirit truly led our paths to cross, so I would learn the truth.* Nick wipes tears that form in his eyes with his thumb and index finger. Nick spends some time in prayer. Nick treks up the bank to his truck and climbs in. He heads to town. Nick parks on a side street and enters the church. He dips his fingers in holy water, makes the sign of the cross, then kneels in the nearest pew, and prays, while waiting for confession.

Nick gets up and is the first one to enter the confessional. He does not even bother to go behind the curtain because he imagines his priest will recognize his voice, though it has been years. Nick sits himself before Father Lyle.

"It has been some time since I have been to confession, Father. My sins are many. To name a few, here goes…I misunderstood something that happened when I was a young man. Because of it, I misrepresented someone for years. I also battle with anger and bitterness…oh, and assumptions." Nick pauses, then, filled with anxiety, he rattles off, "Father, I am ***messed*** up. I have missed Mass for a long time, …and periodically, I have longed for my first love. I do not want to sin against God. I feel like arrows are being shot at me from every direction. I am not worthy to receive the Body of Christ. Because of my assumptions when I was young, I robbed my fiancé and I of a life together. I mislead others about her. I let her down. I did not communicate, nor did I seek truth."

"Nick, God loves you. He wants you to be a part of him and receive Holy Communion. He forgives you of your sins. He is always here for you, Nick. He loves you even when you fall short. The enemy will lie to you. Know God's love is freely given to you. Nothing can separate you from the love of Christ. For your penance…." Father Lyle continues.

Nick prays the Act of Contrition. Father absolves and blesses Nick. Nick feels as if swords are being pulled from his shoulders. He gets up and leaves the confessional and returns to a pew. He kneels and bows his head in prayer. He prays his penance, and offers prayers of thanksgiving. He prays for Nicole.

CHAPTER 20

Zoom Call

Nicole awakens from her nap and hears familiar voices in the kitchen. Nicole walks to the kitchen. "Ah! What a nice surprise!"

Olivia and Lily turn and see their mother.

"We wanted to surprise you this weekend!" Lily smiles.

"We got in about an hour and a half ago. You were napping, so we decided to surprise you with a dessert," Olivia discloses.

Nicole's heart melts. "I love you girls! Thank you!"

"We thought we would ride with you to the wedding tomorrow." Lily places the pie in the oven.

"I like that idea. We will just go to Mass in Careyville," Nicole mentions.

Lily and Olivia smile at their mom.

The Friday afternoon is filled with catching up and some time spent outside. The girls decide they want to drive into town.

"Do you want to go with us?" Lily asks Nicole.

"Not right now, but you girls be safe and have fun. I think I will hang out here. Take a walk. Call my sisters," Nicole outlines.

Lily and Olivia nod. The girls drive into town to do a bit of shopping.

Nicole decides to message her sisters and parents. She requests a zoom call. Everyone happens to be available. Kimberly, Lisa, Seth, and Laurie, greet Nicole on Zoom.

"I love this!" Lisa declares.

Nicole smiles. "Yeah, I thought it would be a great way to visit until we get together!"

"You look good, honey. Is everything alright?" Laurie inquires.

"Thank you. Well, yes, everything is alright. The girls came home earlier today. We will drive together to the wedding tomorrow."

"Oh, wonderful!" Laurie exclaims. "Derek and the entire family will be thrilled to see you all!"

"Yes! We are looking forward to it!" Nicole inhales, then exhales. "Hey, I want to let you know, you are never going to guess…after all these years, I finally encounter Nick," Nicole summarizes.

"I always liked him," Seth comments.

"I know you did, Dad." Nicole smiles.

"Is he still as handsome as ever?" Lisa grins.

Nicole also grins and slightly shakes her head with disbelief. "Even more."

"Aww. I am glad you two finally crossed paths," Kimberly expresses. "Wait, is he still married to Amy?"

"I truly have no idea. My guess is yes," Nicole answers. "My question to you all…is it wrong of me to admire him? I hope to someday marry someone like him. He is such a good man. In his presence, I soften. My heart opens to the idea of having a man in my life. I mean, it cannot be him because he is married. I will not allow my thoughts or heart to lead me into sin. But is it wrong to admire him and hope to marry a good man like him?" Nicole feels perplexed.

"Nicole, I want you to listen and hear my words," Seth requests.

Nicole nods. “Yes. Of course.”

“We will meet people through our entire life that we may find attractive, or that we admire. Maybe we like their voice, maybe their talents. Maybe it is the way a person can make us laugh…we all meet many people that we admire for some reason or another. It is not sinful to want to marry a man like Nick. You were engaged to him once, so it is natural to want a good man, such as Nick. Admiring him and hoping to meet someone like him, is entirely different than lusting after him and coming between he and his wife,” Seth details.

Laurie adds, “And I am sure you find him attractive. I am sure many people do. That does not mean you are in sin. Some people are attractive. Some people attract us. That is how friendships are formed. I trust you will be able to navigate your feelings appropriately, and enjoy a long and healthy, rewarding friendship with Amy and Nick.”

Nicole smiles. “Yes. Exactly. I mean, once in a great while, it still stings he and I did not marry. And yes, he is very handsome, and I am attracted to everything about him. But I have no problem keeping things upright. I just love talking to him. I mean, I have not visited with him much, yet…but I appreciate his friendship. I DO hope I meet someone like Nick. I mean, honestly, I am happy by myself. But when I am in his presence, I soften. My heart opens to the idea of having someone, and I look forward to meeting someone like him.

Each family member smiles at Nicole.

“I am happy you and Nick’s paths crossed. How did that happen?” Lisa asks.

“That’s a story for another day.” Nicole peers at her family on Zoom.

“I am happy for you,” Kimberly expresses. “Anytime you need to visit, just call all of us and one of us. We are all here for you, sis.”

Nicole smiles. “Gosh! I wish I could hug you all right now!”

The family expresses love toward each other.

Seth comments, "You know, your paths may not cross again for a long time. I mean, you have lived it that area sixteen years, and they just now crossed."

"That's true. Well, it would be nice to have an active friendship with him and Amy. Maybe our paths crossed for a reason." Nicole ponders. "Alright, I will see you guys tomorrow! Thank you for letting me share with you!" Nicole voices.

"Of course, that's what families do," Laurie conveys.

CHAPTER 21

Nick Visits his Parents

That Saturday evening, knowing that regardless of the sins and weaknesses of humans, the Holy Blessed Sacrament of Holy Communion remains the body, blood, soul, and divinity, of our Lord Jesus Christ. Nick returns to church, and for the first time in decades, receives the Body of Christ.

After Mass, Nick decides to swing by the local ice cream store and get a gallon of ice cream. He is going to visit his parents. He arrives at his parent's home and carries in the ice cream.

Paul and Emily hear their kitchen door from the garage, open.

"Hey, it's me, Nick. I brought some ice cream," Nick hollers. He sets the ice cream on the counter, grabs three bowls, spoons, and the ice cream scoop.

"Aw, what a nice surprise!" Emily smiles when she enters the kitchen.

"I'll take two scoops," Paul instructs while he pulls out chairs at the table for Emily and himself.

Nick carries over the bowls, spoons, and napkins.

"Amy still out of town?" Emily asks.

"Yes. She will be home Thursday," Nick replies. Nick then glances at both of his parents. "I went to Mass tonight."

Paul swallows a bite of his ice cream. "That is great news!"

"What prompted you to return to church, honey?" Emily inquires.

"Nicole," Nick answers.

"Nicole?" Paul questions.

"Yeah. I met her daughters. Well…it's a long story I will get into it later, but I want to let you know…you guys were right all those years ago. Alex, along with both of you, told me to seek the truth, and not to be led by assumptions. I did exactly the opposite. I made decisions from assumptions. Tormented myself with things that were not even true." Nick recalls the past.

"What do Nicole's daughters have to do with this?" Emily asks.

"I met them. We got to visiting about college. I asked if they had young men in their lives…then, for whatever reason, they felt it necessary to share with me what happened to their mother, Nicole, all those years ago. She was drugged at that party," Nick details.

Somber expressions cast across the faces of Paul and Emily.

"Sounds like the timing was led by the Holy Spirit to reveal the truth to you." Paul dips his spoon into his ice cream.

"Also, I don't think I shared with you, but many years ago, at the ribbon-cutting ceremony for the park at the lake…I ran into Cami," Nick discloses.

"Aww," Emily voices.

"Well, it was nice. I met her husband. Their sons at that time were young. She told me the guy that I thought was Nicole's new boyfriend…was her cousin! They were all over at the Thompson home that weekend for a house warming party." Nick pauses. He lowers his head. "I got that wrong, too."

Paul and Emily both extend their hands to pat their son's arm.

"Anyway, after I found out about Nicole being drugged, I decided I needed to go to confession and return to Mass," Nick informs.

"That is a good thing." Emily smiles.

"Yeah…except…seeing her...well…when I looked into her eyes…it is as if we can still read each other without saying a word. And…it's POWERFUL! How can I be friends with her and not let my hugs get carried away into more? I do not want to sin against God. An affair offers Nicole nothing and launches both of us into sin, plus my feelings are deeper than a lustful encounter. I want to wake up next to her. I want to love and protect her. I would marry her in a heartbeat if I was available. I truly want her in my life…but how does that work? What does that look like?" Nick seeks wisdom.

Paul and Emily glance at each other.

"I'll go first," Emily lovingly voices. "If you shun Nicole, she will feel devastated all over again. Remember, she hurts, too. My guess is she feels the same for you." Emily pauses.

"Oh, I am sure she feels the same. I can *feel* the energy between us when we are next to each other!" Nick jumps in.

Emily nods and continues. "Yes, I am sure you do. But knowing Nicole, she will keep you protectively filed under forever friends and as her brother in Christ so she can hug you, without it leading anywhere. Knowing Nicole, I believe she will want to be friends with both, you, and Amy. I am sure Nicole will want to be a part of your lives, Nick. Now that you have reconnected, do not reject her. You can be friends. I trust you will figure it out."

Nick listens, then peers into the eyes of his dad. "What are your thoughts?"

Paul tilts his head. "Boy, that's tough. You're sure you want Nicole in your life?"

"Yes. One hundred percent!" Nick confirms.

"I thought so. And I understand…I would too. I agree with your mother, file Nicole under forever friends. She is first and always, your sister in Christ. I am sure you will run into her from time to time. Maybe, invite Nicole to lunch with you and Amy. I don't know…I am confident you will be able to manage your feelings. But, Nick…don't ignore Nicole and treat her as an outcast, like she is the other woman. Because, she is not! Knowing Nicole, she does not want to be the other woman. I am sure Nicole is as thankful as you are, to reconnect," Paul details his opinion.

"I am just concerned about keeping my feelings at bay. I mean, honestly, it took everything inside me to restrain myself from kissing her when I saw her. I still feel a deep, natural connection with her. Plus, I need to apologize to Nicole…for everything. Including, for not being there for her when she needed me the most." Nick peers at his parents.

"I am sure you will have an opportunity for all that," Paul assures. "I agree with your mother, do not ignore Nicole. The time we are given is short. You never know when your last day will be, or hers, for that matter. Do you really want to ignore her because you can't handle your feelings? Think of her as your sister in Christ. You will never go wrong," Paul advises. "When your powerful feelings surface, pray for Nicole. Remember, love, is to will the good of the other, for the sake of the other."

"My feelings for Nicole ARE powerful feelings! Sometimes, it is as if I can feel her next to me just from my thoughts." Nick sighs.

"Yes, I imagine they are. You are a loyal, upright man. Everyone wrestles with emotions and feelings. You are not alone," Paul conveys.

"Please, since you cannot be married to Nicole, love and embrace her as your friend, your sister in Christ. Pray for the best for her. Communicate. It will be beneficial to everyone." Emily pats Nick's hand. "Enjoy the moments you are alive with Nicole as your friend."

Nick nods. He rubs his forehead with his fingers. "I can do that. And, I am going to apologize as soon as I get an opportunity."

"That is a good place to start." Emily smiles at her son.

"What do you believe Father would advise you to do?" Paul questions his son.

Nick frowns. "To avoid the near occasion of sin." Nick sighs. "I know what I must do for the good of us all…to behave as a good friend to Nicole. To pray for her and enjoy our time together as siblings in Christ. And manage my feelings. We have already missed out on a lot of life together because of my assumptions. I can love Nicole as my sister, since I cannot have her as my wife." Nick contemplates. "I agree, you are right. It would be wrong to ignore Nicole and treat her as the other woman, when she is not."

Nick and his parents exchange eye contact.

Nick slightly shakes his head. "I'm sure at times it is not going to be easy. Because, I am telling ya, the unspoken energy between us is powerful!"

CHAPTER 22

Going to Town

Nick escorts Amy out to her car. "Did you have a good visit with your parents and Patrick and Simone?"

"I did. What did you do?" Amy smiles.

"Well, I went to confession and attended Mass last Saturday," Nick informs.

"Wow! That's…well, I didn't see that coming," Amy expresses surprise.

"I would like you to join me Saturday," Nick conveys.

Amy shakes her head. "I don't think so. That is one more thing you can do without me."

"That's a problem. I believe we should attend Mass together," Nick expresses.

"Yeah, you said that years ago. Look, my husband, Patrick, and I went to Mass when he was on leave. And I attended Mass regularly until I got word he was killed. It's just not my thing," Amy maintains.

"I don't understand. Seeking God, especially when we are broken, makes sense to me," Nick explains.

"I know. But to me, I feel God let me down." Amy turns to get into her car.

"I *know* you feel that way. I do not understand that mentality at all." Nick places his hands on the top of her open driver's door.

"Look, we both know my true one love is Patrick. Maybe I am still angry God took him. And we know Nicole is your forever love. The one that makes you tick…." Amy outlines.

Nick jumps in. "I think there is more than one person we can truly, deeply love."

"Well, I believe that, too. But you and I both know that we were both products of a lot of traumas in a short time. You stepped in to be my provider and a daddy to Patrick Alexander, whom you raised to be an incredibly strong, faithful man. Without your guidance and the love of your parents and sister and her family…I really do not know if he or I would have done so well. You were a real gift to us, Nick." Amy peers up into Nick's eyes.

"There is something I wanna tell you," Nick communicates.

"Can it wait? I have an appointment," Amy voices.

"It will only take a minute. Nicole and her family live in this county. I found out recently. I was on a medical call to her home," Nick discloses.

"Why are you just now telling me?" Amy quizzes.

"You have been out of town…remember? Visiting Patrick and then over to your parents. I chose to tell you in person," Nick informs.

"Is she alright?" Amy asks.

"Seems to be," Nick answers.

"Maybe you have forgiveness in your heart. I find I don't have much." Amy shrugs. "After what she did to you, I wouldn't give her the time of day."

"Amy, what I believed to be true all these years was incorrect. I did not know the truth. I came to plausible conclusions from assumptions that made sense in my mind at the time, and never sought the facts. And that is on me. I went to confession because I am tired of living with anger, bitterness, resentment…all things that keeps me from enjoying and celebrating life. I need God in my life. I need the healing I believe we all are given, when we receive the Body of Christ. I need the Sacrament of Reconciliation. I do not want to be out of God's grace. Does that mean I will not sin? No, most likely, I will still sin. We all do…but what it means is I will seek God for forgiveness and strength, every day, every week. If I do not forgive others, how can I be forgiven? It is important you return to church. For you. Not for me," Nick details.

Amy repeatedly shakes her head. "Look, we have had a good life. Church is just not for me."

"We do have a good life. But I believe it could be more fulfilling," Nick presses.

"I don't know. Are you going to see Nicole again?" Amy questions.

"I'd like to. But honestly, I am the last person she probably wants to see," Nick states.

"If you want to invite her over for dinner, we can do that. Okay, I must leave so I am not late." Amy reaches for the door.

"I don't know that I will see her to ask her. Her family has lived in this area for many years and you, nor I, even knew," Nick reveals.

"Does she have children?" Amy asks.

"Yes. Two daughters. My guess is around twenty-two, twenty-three." Nick peers into Amy's eyes.

"Well, makes sense. There are many people who live in the county we do not know…even in our community. Plus, Patrick is twenty-eight now, so we would not have even attended the same sporting events through school. Well, if I see her, I will invite her over. I always did like her. And you can tell me the rest of this story when I get home." Amy smiles.

Nick nods and steps away from the car.

Amy arrives at the doctor's office for her scheduled appointment. She is led back to his office. She fears the worst since she is escorted to his office.

"Hello, Amy," Doctor Conrad voices as he enters in through his office door and walks over to behind his desk to sit down.

Amy nods. "Hello, Doctor Conrad." Amy slouches. "Must be bad since you brought me here."

"Where is Nick? I figured he would want to be here," Doctor Conrad asks.

"Oh…." Amy frowns, then misleads. "He is out of town. Yes, he would certainly be here if he knew, I mean if he was in town."

Doctor Conrad's eyebrows furrow. He nods. "I see. Alright. The news is not good. The labs and CT show it is back."

"I see. Is it treatable this time?" Amy leans forward in her chair.

Doctor Conrad slowly shakes his head. "It is not. I am sorry, Amy. I know this is not the news you were wanting to hear."

"It doesn't matter what I want." Amy sighs.

"Of course, it matters. You are a beautiful woman, Amy, with many gifts. Your life matters and is precious in the sight of God," Doctor Conrad heartfully conveys.

Here we go, Amy thinks to herself. "How much time do I have?"

"Only God knows…." Doctor Conrad is interrupted.

"Okay, enough about God! What do you know?" Amy insists.

Doctor Conrad expresses a look of compassion. "What happened to you that hardened you?"

"Um...well, let me think…oh, I know! The love of my life was killed in combat! Then I killed a man in a car accident! And he was to be a priest! Oh…and the boy…well young man I married, was going through grief and heartache. And I *KNEW* he was in love in someone else. I could have encouraged him to find her…but I was selfish. I am pretty sure at this point, God hates me," Amy angrily blurts out then begins to cry.

Doctor Conrad slides the box of Kleenex within Amy's reach. "I have met your son. He is a very kind, wonderful man. He married a lovely girl, and they attend church. I think you did pretty well. You have many gifts, Amy. I am sorry you appear unable to see them. You do know that you are created in the very image of God. Every single strand on your head, he knows. Every thought, every tear. What would your late husband tell you?" Doctor Conrad speaks frankly.

Amy grins and slightly raises her head. "He would tell me he has always been with me. He would tell me he is glad I married Nick. He would thank Nick for being such a good dad to his son, and husband to me. Patrick, my late husband, would tell me to remember all the fun we had and to embrace the life I have." Amy pauses to wipe her eyes and nose. "Thank you, Doctor." Amy stands. "I guess maybe I ***do*** need to see Father Lyle."

Doctor Conrad stands and steps from behind his large mahogany desk. He positions himself in front of Amy. "Five to six months, maybe. You have never told Nick, have you?"

"Okay, thank you for telling me. And…no. Not then…not now," Amy confides.

Amy leaves the office and drives to the store. She parks close to the front door. She thinks about what the doctor told her, along with her conversation with Nick. She shakes her head and gets out of her car. She enters the store, grabs a shopping cart, and begins to stroll the aisles. She rounds the corner and low and behold, there is Nicole.

"Well, what do you know…Nicole Thompson!" Amy voices.

Nicole shifts her eyes from reading a label to a voice she recognizes.

Nicole gasps. "Amy! Wow!" Nicole steps closer to greet Amy with a hug.

"Nick was telling me your family lives in this area," Amy shares.

"Yep…yep we do." Nicole nods. "Well, it's close to the lake, there is a lot of hiking trails…peaceful…."

"I hear ya." Amy inhales and exhales, "Why don't you and your family join us for dinner? Say, Sunday at 4 p.m.?"

"No, I couldn't." Nicole shakes her head.

"Why not? I am sure Nick would like to see you," Amy confirms.

Nicole's facial expression resembles that of someone who has just taken a bite of something unexpectedly sour. "I don't know that I believe that."

"I don't know where you get that idea. We have a lot to catch up on." Amy pauses to swallow. "How many will be coming?"

"Uh, no…I don't think so. Not this week," Nicole stammers.

"Look, the least you can do is come to my home for dinner since you didn't come to our wedding!" Amy teases.

Nicole feels worse. "I am sorry about…."

Amy interrupts, "Don't worry! You did not even KNOW when we got married! How many guests? What's your husband's name?"

Nicole sighs. "It will just be me. My husband passed away eight years ago. My daughters return to college Sunday."

"Oh. I am sorry. I did not know," Amy expresses.

"No. How would you know?" Nicole sighs.

"Well, it's settled. You come to our home Sunday at 4 p.m. No, you do not need to bring anything!" Amy reaches in her purse for a business card and a pen. Amy scribbles down their address on the back and hands the card to Nicole. "See you Sunday. We will catch up then!"

Nicole nods. "Alright. I will be there."

Amy pushes her cart down the aisle. Nicole stands in disbelief. Nicole continues to gather a few items to make a delicious dinner for her daughters.

CHAPTER 23

Saturday Mass

"It's time to leave for Mass. Are you girls ready?" Nicole hollers in the direction of her daughter's bedrooms.

Lily and Olivia come from their rooms. All three ladies have lovely dresses on. They get into Nicole's SUV and leave for church.

"I love this church! Everyone always makes us feel so welcome!" Olivia quietly comments upon entering, after the greeters welcome them.

Nicole smiles. She loves this church as well. The family enters and finds a pew three rows back. The church is beautiful. Olivia is glancing around to see if any of their friends are there. Olivia slightly taps Lily's leg. Lily gives Olivia a curious look. Olivia, again, discreetly taps Lily's leg, and points with the index finger of her right hand hidden beneath her left hand.

Lily rolls her lips and looks in the direction Olivia is pointing. Lily's eyes widen.

"It's him! Lily whispers to Olivia.

"I know!" Olivia whispers back.

Nicole grabs ahold of the pew to rise from kneeling to sit in the pew. When she does, she happens to glance around and she sees Nick Parks. Thoughts rush Nicole. *Oh, my lanta! What is HE doing here? Well, that's a silly question. We have been attending this parish for 16 years and not once have I seen him here on a Saturday night! Nor his parents! Well, last Saturday, I attended another church, due to a wedding...and tonight...they are all here? Lord Jesus...really? Grant me the strength and courage I need. Please heal me. And you know what? It'll be alright. All will be well.*

Nicole and her daughters exchange smiles, like they all know something and wonder if the other one knows.

After Mass, Nicole is hoping to rush out, but that does not happen. People sitting around her, along with others step close to welcome the girls home from college.

Nick, and his parents also work their way over and stand in the aisle waiting to visit with Nicole and meet her daughters.

"Nicole Thompson!" Emily holds out her arms to embrace Nicole and whispers, "We have missed you terribly, honey."

When they release arms, the smile that now decorates Nicole's face does not disappear. Nicole wipes the mist forming in her eyes. Paul extends his arms to Nicole. Nicole and Paul exchange eye contact and then an overdue hug.

"I can see these beautiful girls are your daughters." Emily is always so gracious and kind. "I am Emily. I knew your mother when she was probably younger than you girls."

Lily and Olivia smile.

"Hello, my name is Lily. I am the oldest." Lily gives Emily a hug.

"My name is Olivia. It is nice to meet you both." Olivia also reaches to give Emily a hug.

Paul exchanges a firm handshake with the girls. "This is Nick, our son. He and your mother were…." Paul re-evaluates what he is going to say when he notices the expression on Nick's face. "…good friends."

Nick and Nicole just stare at each other. They both appear to feel kind of awkward, yet, they seem to be very happy.

"Looks like life has treated you well," Nicole comments exchanging eye contact with Nick.

"Are you saying I'm fat?" Nick retorts and winks.

Nicole giggles. "No. You're quite in shape, I am just saying…you look healthy." Nicole turns red.

"To my knowledge, I am." Nick smiles.

"Aw, Nick could always make your mother giggle." Emily smiles with love.

Olivia and Lily grin and exchange a quick glance with one another.

"Tell me, Nicole, how long have you lived in this area?" Paul questions.

Nicole feels terrible now. "Sixteen years." She sighs.

Paul and Emily feel a bit of a sting.

Nicole senses it. "I know. I am so sorry I did not once reach out to you. And apparently, we have been attending the same church all these years, and didn't even know. But now that I see you. Please forgive me. It was wrong of me not to contact you and miss out on all these years. I guess I was afraid."

Emily steps in front of Nicole and swoops her into a loving embrace. "We have made contact now. Let's keep it that way, shall we?"

Nicole nods her head while in the embrace of Emily's hug.

"Honestly, we ***have*** kept track of you. We chose to remain out of your life for the sake of everyone involved," whispers Emily.

"I completely understand," Nicole whispers as they sway.

Nick and the girls exchange eye contact with each other while they observe the exchange between his parents and their mother.

Paul pats Nicole on the back and leans in to whisper while she is still hugging Emily, "There is nothing to forgive. God led us back together, that is what matters. Please…don't be a stranger anymore."

"I won't," Nicole assures. She sniffles.

Emily finally releases their powerful hug, and then places her hands on each of Nicole's arms. "It is so good to see you." Emily leans in and kisses Nicole on the cheek.

Nicole smiles and feels at peace.

Nick addresses the girls, "It is nice to see you both."

"Nice to see you," The girls convey in unison.

"And for the record, you have not seen me here because I only returned to church last weekend." Nick glances at Nicole, her daughters, and his parents.

Nick and Nicole's eyes lock.

"Well, we better go, I made the girls a special dinner since they return to college tomorrow," Nicole explains. "Where is Amy?"

Emily and Paul glance at each other.

"Who is Amy?" Lily asks.

"She is my wife," Nick answers.

Nick raises and lowers his shoulders. He gazes at Nicole. "I don't know if you remember, but she is not a fan."

"Of church?" Lily reacts with surprise.

"Of God?" Olivia questions.

Nick tightens his lips. "Of either."

An expression of perplexity casts across the faces of Nicole's daughters.

"Well, we better go as well." Paul places his hand on the lower part of Emily's back. "It is sure good to see you Nicole, and meet both of you." Paul makes eye contact with Nicole and her daughters.

Paul and Emily lead the others down the aisle and out the double doors of the church. The girls follow, with Nick and Nicole walking side by side.

Nicole leans toward Nick as they trail behind their families. She quietly voices, "Seems a little awkward…."

"Yeah, maybe. But then again…it seems like home," Nick whispers, grins, and shoots a wink at Nicole. He then stops and places his hand in front of her, signaling for her to stop. They stand in the vestibule. The rest of their families have already stepped outside. Nick peers into Nicole's eyes. "Hey, I want to apologize for not seeking out the truth all those years ago. It robbed us of life together. I let my assumptions direct my judgement. I ask you to forgive me. All I have wanted, is the best for you. And, for God to bless us."

Nicole nods, and reaches to move some hair off her face.

"In fact, for any unkind words I have ever said to you, I want to wash my own mouth out with soap!" Nick asserts.

Nicole giggles. "Now, that's funny."

"It's nice to see I can still make you laugh." Nick grins. "It may be funny, but it is true. I am deeply sorry for any unkind words I have spoken…for letting my assumptions get the best of me…which robbed you and I…of our wedding…of our life…." Nick stares into Nicole's eyes.

"It's alright. I forgive you. Those words don't even taste right, I should be the one asking for your forgiveness, for all those years ago." Nicole sighs.

"Nicole, you did nothing wrong. How about we table that conversation for another time? I was so angry at God, the universe, and everything…." Nick confides. "Plus, I am pretty sure, I SHOULD be the one apologizing. As I said, my assumptions caused us to miss out on a LOT of life together. I was not there for you when you needed me most. For everything, I am sorry."

Nicole nods. Nick wraps one arm around the top of her shoulders and gently draws her toward him. They lean in and touch heads. "I will see you another day." Nick takes his arm from around Nicole and reaches to push open the door for her, but as he does, he stops himself. He and Nicole exchange powerful eye contact. It is as if they can read each other's eyes as they did when they were younger.

Nick then opens the door.

"Yes, tomorrow for dinner at your place." Nicole crinkles her face responding to his words, 'I will see you another day.'

"What?" Nick asks.

"Yep, I ran into Amy at the store, first time in all these years. She insists I come over tomorrow for dinner. So, I will be seeing you tomorrow," Nicole outlines.

"Well, alright then." Nick lets the door close behind him after they exit the church.

Nick and Nicole join their families and amble to their cars.

"Wow! That was eventful!" Lily smiles. "And, Mom! Nick is really handsome!"

Images of Nick enters Nicole's thoughts. Nicole recalls how inviting he looks in a pair of jeans, with a long-sleeve denim shirt over a tee-shirt. A grin forms on Nicole's face. "Yeah, he is." An idea enters Nicole's mind. She decides to share with her daughters. "I have a treat for you girls at dinner tonight."

"What is it?" Olivia inquires.

"Let's just say, it's a story I should have maybe shared many years ago." Nicole turns the corner.

"Mom, sometimes, things we want to share…we just don't, until the Holy Spirit leads us," Olivia chimes in from the backseat.

"I think you may be right." Nicole watches for deer as she drives them to their home in the country. "I think it is going to be a story you girls will enjoy." Nicole pauses. "By the way, I noticed you two and Nick chose the words nice to see you, instead of meet you…." Nicole mentions.

"Yeah, we met him when he was about to leave your driveway. It was the Friday we came home for the family wedding in

Careyville that weekend. He said he was following up," Lily details.

"I see." Nicole softly smiles.

During dinner, Nicole, and her daughters each sip on a glass of wine, which is paired with a delicious Italian meal that Nicole prepared. Quiet conversation fills the dining room. Within minutes, the girls are entranced as they listen to the beautiful love story that unfolds as their mother narrates the details of the last track meet of her senior year of high school, and how she met Nick. The girls finally hear from their mother what she experienced when she was young, and the tragedies and trauma that riddled it.

CHAPTER 24

Dinner with Amy & Nick

Nicole types in the address on her phone so her phone maps can take her to Amy and Nick's. She reads that is about fifteen miles away by black top, a twenty-two-minute drive including short bouts on dirt roads. *Why did I agree to this? We were all friends at one time. It'll be alright.* Nicole psyches herself. She offers prayers on the drive over.

Amy greets Nicole at the door. "Welcome to our home, sweet friend."

Nicole smiles at Amy. "Thank you."

Amy holds the door open for Nicole to enter.

"The kitchen is on the right," Amy directs.

Nicole nods, walks down the hallway and turns right. The kitchen and dining area span before her. "This is beautiful! Did you design it yourselves?"

"We did." Amy pats Nicole on the back. "Here, let me give you a proper welcome!" Amy draws Nicole into her arms and hugs her.

"Here, sit down right here." Amy assigns Nicole a seat across from her.

"Can I help?" Nicole offers.

"No, just sit down," Amy instructs.

Nicole chooses to remain standing until Amy and Nick are at the table. Amy carries over the food. Nick carries over wine glasses and a bottle of Chardonnay. Place settings are already set on the table.

"Let's eat, shall we?" Nick suggests. He offers to pour Nicole a glass of wine, but she slightly wrinkles her nose.

"No, thank you. Not really a fan." Nicole gracefully bows out of having a glass.

Nick pours a glass of wine for Amy.

Nicole notices Nick does not pour himself a glass of wine. Nick is aware that Nicole notices. "Hey, I don't like Chardonnay. Plus, I just don't drink…not anymore."

Nicole nods. "What about prayer?"

Nick and Amy exchange a quick glance.

"You lead us." Amy peers at Nicole and insists.

Nicole leads them in prayer. Nicole begins with the sign of the cross, acknowledging in all they do, they seek to do things in the name of the Father, and of the Son, and of the Holy Spirit.

Amy smiles. "Well, eat up. If you want something other than water, let me know."

"No, this glass of water is perfect, thank you," Nicole politely voices. Nicole then cuts into the steak and smiles. "Mm, perfect." She takes a bite. "Oh, thank you so much for dinner."

Amy expresses, "Ha! You haven't even eaten it all."

"No, but I am going to and I can tell you up front, thank you!" Nicole smiles while she chews her food.

Amy nods. "So, Nicole, what brings you to our part of the country?"

"Well, I thought this was my part of the country as well, but moreover, my late husband was senior landscape architect for the company that was hired for major projects throughout the state. He loved this county, so when our daughters were around seven, we moved to the area," Nicole details.

"Are they twins?" Amy asks.

"No, close enough though, thirteen months apart," Nicole shares.

"Wow!" Nick expresses. "Sounds busy."

Nicole smiles. "It was wonderful. My daughters are close, like my sisters and I."

"Did you guys have more children?" Nicole asks.

Amy shakes her head and glances at Nick. "No, just Patrick. He is twenty-eight, married, and has a little boy. They are expecting their second child in a several months."

"Congratulations! How exciting! You're grandparents!" Nicole expresses joy.

Nick and Amy exchange a smile.

"I am so happy for you two," Nicole earnestly voices.

"Well, thanks, Nicole. So, what happened to your husband?" Amy asks. She reaches for the wine bottle and pours herself another glassful.

"He passed away of a heart attack when the girls were in high school," Nicole discloses.

"Aw, I'm sorry to hear that. So, do you date? Where do you live?" Amy rattles off questions.

"About a year after Mark passed, I decided to sell my home and build a home in the country, where I hope to forever live. As for dating, I am a firm believer that once a person finds themselves alone who has been married for a long time, they should remain by themselves at the very least a year." Nicole takes a drink of her water.

"Oh? Why is that?" Amy questions, and swallows another drink of her wine.

Nick, also, is curious as to Nicole's answer.

"Because, in my humble opinion, if you end up by yourself after years of marriage, you need at least year to heal if not more, and equally important, to figure out life by yourself. You must know how to be happy on your own before you can be happy with someone else." Nicole takes another drink of her water and sets it down. "But that is my personal belief."

"And are you happy?" Amy peers at Nicole.

"I am at peace. My heart is full of joy. Am I lonely? Perhaps at times, but not enough to entangle myself. I just have not met the right person yet. I am not opposed to the idea. Mark was a such a good man to our daughters and myself. And since he passed eight years ago, I am writing a new chapter," Nicole explains.

"I think you are onto something. Go, Nicole!" Amy points and articulates. Amy pours herself another glass of wine.

"Enough about me, tell me about you guys!" Nicole expresses eagerness.

"Not much to tell." Nick leans back in his chair.

"What?" Amy glances at Nick and smiles. "Nick worked full time while he went to college, became a paramedic, then a fireman, then was promoted to Fire Chief." Amy shifts her eyes to Nick, "That, is...a big deal, babe. Thank you for taking such good care of Patrick and I." Amy blows Nick a kiss.

Nick nods.

"Wow! That is fantastic, Nick! Congratulations!" Nicole wipes her mouth with a napkin.

"I hope you have enjoyed your life, Amy. What do you like to do?" Nicole expresses interest.

"Oh, yeah...me. Well, let me see, I am Nick's wife." Amy raises her wine glass, then has another drink. "I raised my beloved son-with the help of Nick. We have this beautiful home-thanks to Nick. And I am just wondering why you moved to this area knowing full well Nick and I are here." Amy abruptly becomes cynical.

"What?" Nick shoots Amy a look.

Amy shrugs. "Just wondering, babe." Amy smacks her lips together and stares at Nicole. She raises her almost empty glass of wine, "Do tell...."

"I better go." Nicole scoots her chair back from the table. "Amy, your home is lovely! Dinner was delicious! I thank you very much! It is truly my honor to spend some time with you both." Nicole is gracious.

"So, tell us, why did you leave Nick? I mean, really, you had the best guy, and YOU blew it!" Amy's words are slurred and curt.

Nicole stands. Her eyes widen. "Amy, if I have offended you somehow, I am truly sorry. What happened when we were just out of high school is so many years ago, and I cannot even change what happened ten minutes ago, let alone decades. And honestly, it is between Nick and I. I do hope to see you again, on better terms."

"Oh, I KNOW what happened! Nick told me everything! I helped heal him! Not you!" Amy continues to blurt out drivel and grimace.

Nick's eyes almost pop out. He too, stands, and glances at Nicole. "I'll see you out."

"Of course, you will." Amy smirks and pours herself the last of the wine from the bottle.

"I hope to see you again, Amy. Thank you, so much for inviting me. Take care," Nicole offers heartfelt sentiments.

Nick discreetly places one hand on Nicole's mid-back, positions himself almost directly behind her. He quickly escorts her to the door.

When they reach the door, Nick steps in front of Nicole and opens the large, wooden front door for Nicole. They exchange eye contact.

"I am so sorry, Nicole. I am very embarrassed. Don't hold it against her, she means well," Nick explains.

"Nick, please do not feel embarrassed for her behavior. It is not a reflection of you. It reflects what is in her heart. It sounds like she has anger and grudges, and it most likely stems from her husband being killed during his tour," Nicole rationalizes. "It is a lack of allowing God's love into her life." Nicole's lips tighten.

"Maybe, but she has no right to take it out on you, and for that, I am sorry," Nick offers.

"Thank you. It is alright." Nicole and Nick peer into the eyes of each other.

"Drive safe, Nicole," Nick requests.

"I will, thank you." Nicole steps down the front porch and walks to her car. She drives home. Sadness overwhelms Nicole. She prays for Amy's broken heart.

That evening, Nick carries Amy to bed, as he has done many times through their life together. He gently lays her in their bed, and takes her shoes off. Nick is none too pleased about how Amy behaved to Nicole. Nick thinks to himself, *Can I blame her? I misrepresented Nicole all these years. Father, forgive me.* Nick happens to glance down and notices a pill bottle on the floor. He picks it up and recognizes the prescription. He realizes Amy is hiding the cancer is back. He places the bottle back where he found it.

CHAPTER 25

Apologies & Healing

"I sure wish you would go to Mass with me." Nick smiles at Amy. "It is kind of embarrassing to attend Mass without my wife."

"Nick, me not going is not a reflection of you at all. You should NOT be embarrassed. Please don't be. Me not going reflects where my heart and beliefs are, not yours. Nobody knows my life. If they want to be judgy, they can be," Amy contends.

"Amy, nobody is judgy of you. Everyone I know thinks you are a superstar! And, you are right, I should go regardless of your personal choices and not let your choice effect mine," Nick articulates.

"Exactly. You should go because of your belief, and do not let mine keep you from it. As far as a superstar, I don't know." Amy shrugs.

"Are you kidding? I look at you and think, WOW! You were a major player in getting programs for widows of veterans with children established in this area. You helped with the school when

Patrick attended. You are a source of strength for everyone who meets you," Nick affirms.

"Yeah, and I was pretty trashy to Nicole." Amy shrugs.

Nick nods. "That too."

Amy tightens her lips. "Do you think she will forgive me?"

"I know she will," Nick assures.

Later that week, Amy hopes to run into Nicole. She knows Nicole likes to go to the grocery store on Fridays. Amy parks and goes into the store. She methodically wanders the aisles hoping Nicole will show up. Amy turns the aisle and there is Nicole. They are facing each other.

Both ladies remain silent.

"Thank you, again, Amy for a delicious meal," Nicole breaks the ice.

"Oh, it was truly, my pleasure." Amy smiles. "Nicole, will you find it in your heart to forgive me for being such a bitter, callose woman to you?"

Nicole reaches her hand out and places it on the top of Amy's hand. "Of course."

"So, you forgive me?" Amy questions.

"Yes. Naturally." Nicole lovingly smiles.

Amy sighs. "You do? Can you just say it, so I hear it?"

"Of course, Amy. I forgive you," Nicole states.

"Thank you. I appreciate that." Amy nods.

"Can I speak directly?" Nicole questions.

"I hope you always speak directly," Amy states.

"I do, but I feel I have to walk on eggshells around you," Nicole explains.

"I know. But don't. Give it to me straight." Amy slightly grins.

"A few minutes back, you requested I say the words I forgive you," Nicole voices.

"Yeah, I guess." Amy shrugs.

"You mentioned…so you could hear it. Forgiveness Amy. It is key to love, health, healing. WHY…are you waiting?" Nicole boldly communicates.

"Waiting for what?" Amy quizzes.

"To return to the Sacrament of Reconciliation, receive forgiveness, and receive the Body of Christ in the Blessed Holy Eucharist. Is what is keeping you from receiving the Body of Christ, greater than the Body of Christ? You don't have to answer me, just think about it," Nicole evangelizes.

Amy cannot believe Nicole has challenged her and boldly spoken to her. She ponders, *maybe the Holy Spirit has moved Nicole to speak to me.*

"Amy, you are a beautiful soul. If something is keeping you from receiving the Holy Body and Blood of Our Lord Jesus Christ, you need to address it. I would love to see you and Nick at Mass. You guys are my family. I love you guys. It has been years, but in the realm of forever friends, time has no minutes. Just think about it. You expressed to me you wanted me to forgive you. Think of how relieved that made you feel…and I am only human. Think how you will feel if you ask our Creator of the Universe, Our Father in Heaven, to forgive you," Nicole campaigns for her sister in Christ, to return to Mass.

Amy is astounded. She completely understands and hears the words Nicole speaks. "Thank you, Nicole. You have given me a lot to contemplate.

Nicole hugs Amy. "I love you, Amy."

"I love you, Nicole." Amy smiles.

Later that day, Amy decides to go to the parish. She does a search on her phone to find out when the confession times are. Amy arrives early. She hopes she will be the first in line, not to be first, but to be sure she has enough time. When Amy arrives, she is thankful no one else is in line behind her since she is concerned about taking up a lot of time. She ponders, *perhaps I should have made an appointment.* Amy walks in and just sits down in front of Father. She does not remember any of the protocol or prayers. Amy stares at Father. "Forgive me, I do not even know where to start." Amy lowers her head, pauses, and raises her head. "It has been decades since I have been to confession or communion."

Father points to an 8 x 10 laminated sheet with the appropriate prayers.

Amy slightly feels relief. "Thank you, Father." Amy lists off all the sins she can remember, asks for forgiveness for those she cannot remember, and adds her recent ones of falling short of being kind and virtuous.

After the Sacrament of Reconciliation is complete, Amy stands and thanks Father again, then exits the confessional, finds a pew, and prays her penance.

The next day, Nick hollers down the hall, "I will be leaving for Mass soon." He reaches for his water jug and fills it. He turns and sees Amy. "Wow, you look nice, where are you going?"

"I thought I would come to Mass with you…if that is alright. Your parents have switched to Saturday evening Mass, haven't they?" Amy smiles.

"They have. Sure, of course it is alright." Nick screws the lid on his jug. "Um, ya know…." Before Nick finishes his comment, Amy speaks.

"Yes, I went to confession yesterday. I am good to receive the Sacrament of Holy Communion," Amy informs.

"Well, that is great!" Nick opens the door for Amy to the garage. "Can I ask what has moved you to return?" He opens the passenger side door of his truck for Amy.

She climbs in. "For one thing, Nicole. I saw her yesterday in the store. I sought her out to apologize for my atrocious behavior at dinner…and she was so gracious to me. So, kind." Amy grins, "So, bold."

"That's great! She has always seemed to have a natural ability to evangelize…kind of like Alex." Nick taps the garage door opener, turns the truck on, and drives out. He too, backs in his vehicle.

"Oh, yes! Exactly." Amy nods with peace.

"Aaaand?" Nick asks.

"And what?" Amy replies.

"What's the other thing?" Nick questions, as he turns out of their drive onto the dirt road.

"Oh, that. Well, that one is between me and God," Amy conveys.

"Fair enough." Nick stops at the stop sign before he turns onto the highway.

Amy and Nick sit next to his parents. Nicole sits across the aisle a few rows forward.

After Mass, Nick, Amy, Paul, and Emily make their way over to Nicole.

"I am so glad we have switched to this Mass time. We get to see you every Saturday." Emily hugs Nicole.

Nicole smiles. "Thank you."

"Nicole, I insist, sit with us. You are family to us all. At least, sit with us sometimes," Amy extends an invite.

Nicole smiles. "Thank you. Maybe I will, sometimes."

Conversations are enjoyed as they stroll out of church.

Amy grabs ahold of Nicole's hand. "Come mere." Amy pulls Nicole into a hug. "Thank you, Nicole. Your words made sense, your love, genuine. I should have returned years ago."

Nicole smiles. "It is my pleasure, Amy. I am glad to be a part of your life."

"Always." Amy lovingly smiles.

CHAPTER 26

The Following Months

The following week after Mass, Amy rushes to Nicole. "I have a huge favor."

"Name it," Nicole requests.

"I know this may sound a little weird, but honestly, we have missed out on so much! When do your daughters come home?" Amy inquires.

"They are coming home next weekend," Nicole replies.

The two ladies continue to stroll toward the double doors. "Would you please invite your parents, your sisters and their families, along with Nick's parents, Nori and her family, to a gathering?" Amy smiles. "I know this is a big ask, but I want everyone together, to renew old friendships and forge new ones."

Nicole slightly nods her head, "I guess I can do that. I am having my family over anyway since the girls will be home."

"Oh, excellent! Thank you so much, Nicole! I will help prepare food and purchase half of the meal," Amy insists.

"If this will make you happy…." Nicole comments.

"Oh, yes! You have no idea! Okay, also, after next weekend, I really want a Sunday dinner for as many of our family members that can make it. Every Sunday…at least for a few months. I know both you and Nick grew up with Sunday family dinners. Of course, this will just be on a larger scale. I do not want to waste another minute of time. Please, say yes!" Amy requests with exuberance.

Nicole grins. "I can see how happy you are about this idea. Alright, I will talk to Emily and my mom, maybe we can all take turns hosting," Nicole suggests.

"Love it! Our home as well!" Amy offers.

Amy gives Nicole a huge hug. "You have no idea what this means to me! Thank you!"

Nicole smiles and graciously replies, "It is my pleasure. I like the idea of my daughters, your son, my sisters…everyone, getting to know each other. This is really a great idea, Amy." Nicole also feels lost time of missing out with Nick's parents and sister.

As planned, the families alternate homes every Sunday for the next few months. The families enjoy conversations, sharing recipes, telling stories, playing games, partaking in excellent food, and talking about the Lord. Amy's idea, though possibly driven by a need inside her, is filling the lives of the families. They each experience a deeper sense of belonging and are grateful for the opportunity to get to know each other.

Over the next several months, every person notices Amy's deteriorating appearance. Amy passes it off as eating something that did not agree with her, but Nick knows, and Nicole suspects. As do both sets of parents.

"I'd like to make a toast," Amy raises her glass of wine. The others raise their glass of whatever they are drinking as well. "To

Nick and his family, for taking me and my son, Patrick, in as their own…for loving us as their own. To Nicole, for showing me love in that hospital bed years ago, right after I delivered Patrick, and for being my friend even when I was not kind to her. Nicole remained steadfast and her words opened my spirit to returning to church. And to all of you, for participating in this endeavor. I approached Nicole to help organize it because I knew that is how your families grew up. I wanted to experience being a part of both of your families. Thank you, all, for gifting me with getting to know each of you. These past few months have been a true blessing…you'll never know. To the words Nicole spoke to me, 'in the realm of forever friends, time has no minutes'." Amy lowers her glass.

Every person in the room expresses in unison, "In the realm of forever friends, time has no minutes."

Emily and Laurie, along with the others, communicate a toast of thanks to Amy and comment on how much they enjoy these Sunday gatherings, paired with how much they love Amy.

Amy feels faint. Nick darts to her side and sweeps her into his arms. He swiftly carries her to his truck and rushes her to the emergency room.

CHAPTER 27

Time Passes

Father Lyle visits the home of Nick and Amy. He prays the last rites over Amy. After Father prays with Amy, Nick escorts him to the door. "Thank you, Father."

"I am honored to serve. Peace dwell within you." Father leaves.

Nick closes the front door and returns to the room Amy is resting comfortably in.

"We did it. We may not have been physically attracted to each other, and I know I sure made life hell for you at times, but we did it. You are right, I should have returned to church years ago. Not shortly before my death…but I am thankful for the time I have had. Thank you for being a good husband to me and father to my son…our son." Amy reaches for Nick's hand.

Nick is quiet. Sorrow fills him. Memories trigger more sorrow.

"I want you to promise me something," Amy barely audible, voices.

"What's that?" Nick asks.

"Aren't you suppose to say, 'Anything'?" Amy grins, though she has no energy.

"Alright. Anything, what is it?" Nick complies.

"I want you to marry Nicole. Do not let anything stand in your way. It may not be perfect at times, but show up for her and communicate for goodness sakes! Promise me! You have my blessing! Patrick, my beloved first husband, and I, agree," Amy details.

"Oh, you talk to him, do you?" Nick chuckles.

Amy smiles from ear to ear. "You know that I do. Anyway, Nick, you have been a perfect husband to me and father to Patrick, do not ever doubt yourself. I know we came together because of tragedies and traumas, but we did it. Now, please, go make Nicole your wife. Protect and love her as you had always planned to." Amy pulls Nick's hand to her lips and kisses the top of his hand.

"I don't know that she will have me. Please don't ask this of me." Nick stares into the eyes of his wife.

"She will." Amy blinks. "Be persistent. God led us all back to each other." Amy smiles and closes her eyes. Amy whispers, "Promise me."

"I'll try." Nick shakes his head. "Let's just focus on you right now."

"Say you will," Amy insists, though her eyes remain closed.

Nick feels confused. He also is experiencing stress, and great anxiety. Nick decides to comply to his wife's wishes and quietly voices, "I will."

Feeling exhaustion, Amy manages to slightly smile. "See, that wasn't so hard. Thank you, Nick. For giving me a good life, and, for agreeing to make Nicole your wife."

"I can't promise that, Amy. I know I said I will…but…I don't know," Nick communicates.

"I know. I am merely assuring you that you have my blessing," Amy acknowledges. "You know, I kept things from you," Amy confesses.

"I know you did," Nick confides.

Amy conveys, "Thank you for not prying."

Nick nods and squeezes her hand.

Patrick enters the room with his wife, Simone.

Nick stands and leans over to kiss Amy's forehead. "Patrick and Simone are here. I will leave you with them now." Nick places his hand tenderly on Amy's cheek.

Amy barely smiles.

Patrick steps next to his mother and weeps. He lays his head onto her stomach.

She musters enough strength to place her hand on his head. "I love you, baby."

Patrick wraps one arm around his mother. "I love you."

Simone steps to the other side of the bed and places her hand on Amy. Nick carries in Chase.

"Gamma!" Chase reaches to touch Amy.

Emily and Paul along with Nick's sister Nori, her husband Derek, and children, Samantha, and Peter, have already said their goodbyes.

Nick carries Chase out of the room.

"Oh, here, Chase. Come and play with your cousins." Emily takes the hand of Chase and leads him to the family room where Samantha and Peter are. Nick returns to the bedroom.

Simone kisses Amy and whispers, "I love you, mom." Simone then departs the room to join the other family members.

Patrick and Nick sit on each side of the bed. They each hold a hand of Amy's. They offer prayers. Family comes and goes while Patrick and Nick remain vigilant by Amy's side. She never opens her eyes again and passes twenty-seven hours later.

Emily peeks in. She steps out and calls the funeral home, and of course Father Lyle. Arrangements that were discussed, have been made.

Several days after the funeral Mass and luncheon, Nick is preparing dinner.

Patrick enters the kitchen. “You never loved her! You did not even know she had cancer! Not the first time…not this time!” Patrick weeps.

Nick moves from the other side of the island to stand next to Patrick. “Son, I knew both times. But, for whatever reason, your mother wanted to hide it from me. I knew it when she had it the first time. I honored her privacy, pretending I didn’t know. And this time, well, I was pretty hurt she still didn’t share with me. But, I respected her wishes, and pretended I had no clue.”

“You knew? Both times?” Patrick wipes his eyes.

“Well, yeah. Of course. How can you live with someone and not know when they are ill? When their weight fluctuates, when they are sick, when their smell is off? Of course I knew,” Nick maintains.

Patrick grabs Nick and squeezes him. “Thank you for telling me. I had it all wrong when I was a kid…and this time as well. I guess I assumed. Thank you for protecting my mother’s secret and not letting her know you knew.”

“Ya know, before your mother passed she informed me that she kept things from me. I told her I know. She conveyed, ‘Thank you.’” Nick reaches in a drawer. “Here, she wrote you a letter.” Nick hands Patrick an envelope.

Patrick sits on a bar stool at the island, opens the letter, and begins to read almost a diary of her life with Nick. The letter recounts when she met Nicole and Nick when they were young. How the couple brought a bouquet and thoughtful gifts to her hospital room after the car accident. Nick observes Patrick’s expressions as he reads the informational, heartfelt letter. “Yeah, I knew Mother was older than you and Nicole. Six years…apparently. I just never gave it much thought. She and my dad married when they were both eighteen, before he left to the military. They were stationed at a base in the United States for a few years before he was deployed. During one of his leaves, they created me. Wow…." Patrick continues to read. "Just wow! I didn't realize Nicole played such an intricate role in getting Mom to return to church!" Patrick continues to read.

Nick remains silent and sips on his water.

Simone walks into the kitchen after she lays Chase down for a nap.

"Come mere." Patrick holds out one arm. Simone steps next to him. He wraps his arm around her. "Read this letter that mom wrote to me. I know what we should name our little girl."

"Oh, what's that?" Simone respectfully questions.

"Amy Nicole Chambers," Patrick announces. "Amy, after my mother, and Nicole, who, from reading this letter, has always left a positive impact on my mother."

Simone gazes into her husband's eyes and softly voices, "I like that. Amy Nicole it is." Simone and Patrick wrap their arms around each other. "Have you read this letter?" Patrick looks at Nick.

Nick nods. "I have. I would like to reread it."

"Sure. In fact, let's make a copy, that way you can keep a copy here, and I will take this one home with me and place in my bible," Patrick suggests.

"Sounds like a solid plan." Nick nods.

"Did you know she wants you to marry Nicole?" Patrick asks.

Nick nods again. "I'm aware. She made me promise her…of course, I don't know…and I do not know if Nicole will have me. I probably damaged our relationship when we were young…from assumptions, I might add." Nick peers into the eyes of Patrick.

"Wait, didn't my mother write in her letter about forgiveness and other relatable topics?" Patrick asks.

"She did." Nick nods.

"There ya go, Dad. You have my mother's blessing, and my blessing. Like mom said in her letter, communicate!" Patrick grins. His arm remains wrapped around his wife.

Simone smiles at Nick.

"Alright. Let me process one thing at a time," Nick requests, and motions with his hands.

"Yeah…of course." Patrick hugs Simone.

"Okay, well, we will be out of your hair tomorrow. We will leave around six in the morning," Patrick communicates.

"Alright, I'll cook us a family dinner tonight. I invited my parents to join us," Nick informs.

"Yes. We look forward to it!" Patrick smiles.

"I love your grandparents," Simone voices to Patrick.

The family enjoys a delicious family meal and conversations. After Chase is tucked in bed, the adults play some cards. They experience bonding through reminiscing and laughter. More family memories are made.

CHAPTER 28

Summer

Time mourning Amy seems to quickly pair with celebrating the new life of her grandchild. Simone gives birth to a beautiful baby girl two months after Amy passes. Patrick and Simone name her, Amy Nicole Chambers.

Nicole sees Nick and his parents at Mass. Nicole's daughters continue to come home from college when they can. Nicole also busies herself with her parents coming out for family dinners, along with her sisters, and their families. Sometimes, Nicole travels to visit them. Life is full and busy for everyone.

Nick's parents and Nicole's parents enjoy the active renewal of their friendship and fun activities they do together.

The families continue to have Sunday get togethers at least twice a month.

One Sunday, when Lily and Olivia are home, along with Patrick and Simone, Lily has an idea.

Lily whispers to Olivia.

Olivia lights up.

"Excuse us." Lily and Olivia stand and leave the family room.

"Do you think mom will care?" Olivia asks.

"She may, but shouldn't everyone here see mother's work? It tells a story of all of them. Everyone in our family, including Patrick, his wife and children have been drawn," Lily insists.

"I agree. Alright." Olivia grabs one box while Lily grabs another. The girls return to the family room.

Seth stands to help his granddaughters. "What do you have here?"

"Oh. No, girls. Nobody wants to see these." Nicole stands.

Lisa and Kimberly get up and walk to the table where the boxes are set by their nieces.

"Mom has drawn pictures of all of us. Her pictures are like a diary of her life. A portrait of everyone in this room is held within these boxes," Olivia voices.

Everyone gathers around. Nicole blushes.

Nick steps next to Nicole and whispers, "They are proud of you. I am proud of you."

The family members take turns admiring the beautiful drawings that capture each of them. Every person reminisces after viewing Nicole's landscape art she has drawn of vacations, along with portraits.

"Oh, honey, these are just beautiful," Laurie comments.

Paul grins. "Ha! You captured my attempts trying to still ski. That's funny. Thank you, Nicole. You have a real gift."

Conversations continue throughout the Sunday gathering.

One day, later in the summer, Nicole is at home. She is preparing dinner. She is waiting for her family to arrive. Nicole hears a knock at the door. She wonders who arrived early and opens the door. Nicole glances and then looks down. She sees Nick before her, kneeling on one knee, gazing up at her.

"Look, I know that you believe people should remain by themselves for some time when they become single. Due to my shortcomings, well, mainly immaturity and lack of communication, not to mention my assumptions, you and I missed out on a lotta life together. I believe we both have experienced healing over these sixteen months. We have also gotten reacquainted and caught up. I can just look in your eyes…no words necessary. I will love and protect you. Will you marry me, Nicole Elizabeth?" Nick opens a ring box that holds a beautiful rose gold band sporting a stunning marquise diamond in the center, surrounded by little diamonds. Nick has kept this ring in his drawer at his parent's house all these years.

Nicole lights up! "Nick! Yes!" Nicole declares.

Nick stands and reaches for Nicole's left hand. He slides the beautiful engagement ring on her ring finger of her left hand. They gaze into each other's eyes. Nick gently leads Nicole into his arms and finally kisses Nicole after all these years. They step back to look into the eyes of each other.

"I love you Nicolas Charles Parks!" Nicole voices.

"And I love you." Nick squeezes Nicole's hands.

They both giggle.

"You remember all those words I said years ago that you mentioned could be vows?" Nicole inquires.

"I believe I do. It was a LOT of words." Nick grins.

Nicole stares into the eyes of Nick. "Yeah…I like our silent communication."

"I do too." Nick kisses Nicole's forehead.

Nicole blushes. "And this ring? How did you know?"

"Well, this is the original engagement ring I purchased for you all those years ago, it came with matching wedding bands for you and I. I recently took the set to the jeweler to have a larger marquise replace the original one, and size up your band and my band."

Nicole is astonished by the details, energy, and thoughtfulness that went in to planning this. "How did you know my size?"

Nick smiles. "I asked Lily and Olivia to measure a ring they know that fits your ring finger."

"You know, I am sweet on you," Nick voices.

Nicole blushes again. “I love hearing your voice.”

“You do realize…we don’t even need words.” Nick leans his forehead into Nicole’s forehead.

“We don’t,” Nicole lovingly whispers.

The two embrace and passionately kiss during their long-awaited reconnection.

Nick and Nicole complete the necessary requirements to marry at their parish. The couple are ecstatic when they find out they can be married October, 15th. It may not be their original date, but they are very thankful a Saturday in October is available. Every person in both families is thrilled with delight!

Nick asks Patrick to be his best man. Nicks requests Aaron Monroe, Alex’s brother, to be his groomsman.

Nicole’s sisters, Lisa and Kimberly, are of course, the ladies that stand up with her. And Cami, well, Cami wants to be the event planner, and she is an outstanding one at that!

Laurie saved Nicole’s wedding dress from all those years ago. The seamstress makes the necessary adjustments so the beautiful satin, lace gown fits.

At the reception, Paul, Emily, Seth, and Laurie stand to the side. Their hearts are full of gladness.

“Cheers! To all things coming full circle after sharp turns,” Paul begins.

“Yes…tragedies,” Emily adds.

“And traumas,” Seth voices.

“To love, finding its way.” Laurie glows.

The parents cast their eyes upon their adult children, who are enjoying their first dance as Mr. and Mrs. Nicolas Parks. They beam from a deep sense of joy.

“They have come a long way to get here.” Paul recognizes.

Seth nods. “They have, indeed.” Seth pats Paul on his mid-back.

Laurie and Emily wrap their arms around each other’s waists.

After the first dance, the parents and guests join the couple on the dance floor. The celebration is as wonderful as the wedding was lovely.

CHAPTER 29

An Autumn Morning

Nick, sporting green and blue plaid cotton pajama bottoms, carries a mug of pumpkin-spice coffee onto the balcony. Nicole is wrapped in an extremely soft, sage-green, over-sized blanket. Nick sets the mug down on the wide ledge of the balcony. He wraps his arms around Nicole's waist. Nicole leans her head onto his shoulder.

"Mm, I sure like waking up to you." Nick nestles into Nicole.

"Mm, and I sure like going to sleep in your arms," Nicole whispers.

The two remain in the comfort of their arms, while viewing across the landscape from the balcony.

They lift their heads and look into the eyes of each other.

"I sure do love you, Mrs. Parks," Nick quietly voices.

"And, I sure do love you, Mr. Parks." Nicole's eyes light up.

"Do you still want to travel to the mountains together?" Nick asks.

"I love that idea!" Nicole leans her head onto Nick's shoulder. "I have been waiting since we were young!

"We leave tomorrow," Nick announces.

"Oh, Nick! I can't wait to be there together!" Nicole exclaims.

"That's what I like to hear," Nick expresses.

In the morning, Nick and Nicole load their truck. They head to the mountains for a three-week adventure! Everything Nicole was wanting to experience with Nick when they were young, they now enjoy. After a delicious dinner, and watching the night unfold on the back deck of the cabin they rented, they settle in for the evening.

"So, how 'bout you tell me a story?" Nicole kisses Nick.

"Alright, I can do that." Nick's heart is full of joy. "Where did I leave off all those years ago? How about I start with, all trails lead to you?"

"Mm, that is a great place to begin…." Nicole gazes into the eyes of Nick.

During their three-week journey, Nick and Nicole bask in their love. The couple enjoy hiking the mountain trails, or four-wheel excursions. Their spirits experience a deep peace and healing when the sounds and scents at the river's edge surround them. They hear the crackles from the campfire, and observe luminous stars adorning the night sky. Nick and Nicole communicate unspoken words with their eyes. The three-week getaway is time well spent.

They awaken to another morning of invigorating, crisp mountain air. While the couple load their truck, they realize the time they lost out on, matters significantly less, than the moments they have now.

Days turn into nights, which rolls into months, that revolves into years. During this time, Nick and Nicole attend Mass together, enjoy family gatherings, communicate, travel, and celebrate their friendship and love.

"You know, not only do I love you, I am sure sweet on you." Nick winks.

Love envelopes Nicole. "Not only do I love you, Nicolas Charles Parks, I just wanted to hear your voice."

Nick and Nicole exchange smiles.

"You know, we don't even need words...." Nick sweeps some hair from Nicole's forehead with his left hand.

"No, we do not." Nicole smiles with love at Nick. "Not then...not now."

The couple turns around, wraps their arms around each other, and stroll back inside, arm in arm, from the balcony. Nick and Nicole crawl into their king size bed. They snuggle in the love and comfort they find in the arms of each other. Nick is about to quietly tell Nicole a story, when she reaches her arm over the side of the bed. She then pulls her arm back with a wrapped gift. She hands it to Nick.

Nick stares with wonder at Nicole. Nick carefully tears the paper away. Before him is a beautiful portrait of him and Nicole gazing into each other's eyes. Mountains are the background. Nick is astounded. "Nicole...this is incredible!"

Nicole shines with joy.

"I am so proud of you!" Nick kisses Nicole. After Nick studies the detailed portrait, he carefully turns the framed drawing over to read the title, *"Our Eyes can read Our Hearts."* Nick is speechless. After a few moments of studying the portrait, he sets the framed drawing securely off the bed. He then leans onto his side to face Nicole. He caresses her face. "I cannot even begin to tell you how much I love you! I thank God we are together!"

"Me too." Nicole smiles.

They passionately kiss and enjoy their physical intimacy.

Nick and Nicole fall asleep peacefully, thankful for another day together.

The End.

I hope you enjoyed this story

Alexandria Chiaro spent her childhood and adolescent summers traveling through beautiful mountain states with her parents. During this time, she began writing poems, songs, and lyrics, which later transitioned into writing short stories.

Many years later, an idea for a title came to her while attending church with her mother. However, it was not until an additional three years later that someone asked about the characters in her story, unlocking the treasure chest to an epic fantasy series that has captivated readers. The three books that are so far in her fantasy series have periodically hit the Most Popular list on Amazon. While taking a brief break from writing in her popular, epic fantasy series, an idea for this drama-romance came to her. Alexandria hopes you will enjoy the love story written in the pages of, To Love, Finding its Way.

Sharing her imaginative stories with you brings Alexandria great joy.

Alexandria fills her time with church, family, friends, fur babies, work, writing, and projects. She greatly enjoys the outdoors along with mountains, & rivers, just as she did those summers long ago.

Enjoy!

www.ingramcontent.com/pod-product-compliance
Lightning Source LLC
LaVergne TN
LVHW090523110826
845146LV00003B/955

* 9 7 9 8 9 8 7 3 1 7 9 6 9 *